STORMY NIGHTS

A Collection of Short Stories

Jules Jones and Storm Duffy

Published by
NineStar Press
PO Box 91792
Albuquerque, New Mexico, 87199
www.ninestarpress.com

Warning: This book contains sexually explicit content, which is only suitable for mature readers.

Print ISBN # 978-1-947139-52-7
Cover by Natasha Snow
Edited by BJ Toth

Table of Contents

Jules Jones

Storm Duffy

Sex and love, lies and truth, shades in between. Happy endings and might-have-beens. Nine tales of these things between men.

Gone Fishing

Mike's doctor prescribed a few weeks on a lonely beach as a rest cure for a weary mind. But even if the beach is empty, the sea holds more than fish.

Naked

Just how far will a man go to understand his partner's desires? Will he bare all – including all of his skin to the razor blade?

One Size Fits All

Hugh's everything that Gavin could ask for in a lover. Everything, apart from his taste in underwear. It's boring. So Gavin decides to rummage through Hugh's underwear drawer—and what he finds is so interesting that he tries it out for size.

The Fraudster

A forensic accountant's job offer to a computer fraudster fresh from prison is a second chance for both.

A Sparrow Flies Through

High tech cottaging provides a few moments of light and warmth on a dark cold night.

If I Offered Thee a Bargain

Just one night of your life in exchange for seven years of love. Would you pay the price?

Jack never dreamed that a reluctant trip back to his home town would thrust him into the world of the sidhe. He finds that the legends are true, but the sidhe have changed.

Any Port in a Storm

A spilt coffee at the tram station on a snowy night leads to a table set for three.

Car Wash

Colin had always loved washing the neighbour's car for pocket money. Rod's classic car collection was a boy's dream. And so is Rod, now Colin's home from university and not a boy any more. Colin's had a little fantasy about Rod's vintage Jaguar and her gleaming curves for a while now...

JULES JONES

GONE FISHING

IT ALL STARTED with a stroll along a private beach. Well, it started further back than that, with why I was strolling along a private beach. My doctor told me to choose between making still more money on my Internet start-up, or living long enough to enjoy the money I'd already made. I took her advice, sold my company, and spent part of the proceeds on a house on a nice, warm isolated beach. Peace and quiet to unwind, enjoy the money I'd made, and maybe come up with another "must have" concept. As it turned out, my timing was perfect, getting out just before the dot-com bubble burst, but I'd needed to get out anyway. I'm no entrepreneur, just a scientist who got lucky with a bright idea. The pressure was doing things to my mind.

Which is why I didn't believe my eyes when I saw the mermaid.

Beautiful, she was, sitting there on the edge of the rock pool. Beautiful and impossible. I thought it was a trick of the bright sunlight, dazzling my eyes. As I got closer, that explanation got harder to clutch onto. She looked real and so did that damned tail. She looked up at me and smiled and spoke. "Hello, man."

The prosaic greeting steadied my nerves, if not my legs. I sat down before I fell down, close enough to touch her tail. It was flesh, not a costume. "You're real."

"Of course I'm real."

"You can't be." Well, not unless some biology research team hadn't bothered sending a truly spectacular paper on genetic engineering to *Nature*. "You're a mermaid. They don't exist."

"Yes, we do." She giggled. "We just went away for a while."

So there I was, sitting on a rock, talking to something that didn't exist. Fine. People pay good money for chemicals to achieve this sort of experience, or so I'm told. I decided to enjoy it and worry about my sanity later. One of the nice things about being independently wealthy is being considered eccentric, not nutty as a fruitcake. Nobody would bat an eyelid if I went home, called a friend, and said, "Hey, I met a mermaid today."

"All right, mermaid. Where did you go, and why have you come back?"

"My name's Pearl, not mermaid. And we haven't come back." She leaned towards me and dropped her voice a little. Nice voice, especially with that huskiness. "Actually, I'm not supposed to be here. But I wanted to see what the land was like. I've heard so many stories about it."

"My name's Mike." I held out a hand. "Pleased to meet you, Pearl." The name seemed a remarkable cliché, but I refrained from commenting. No need to hurt the lassie's feelings even if she was a figment of my imagination.

She looked at my hand, looked back at my face, and then very gingerly shook my hand. Hers felt cool and damp, but otherwise human. "You're not what I expected."

"What did you expect?" I asked.

"Well, I knew you might not believe in me. We've been away for such a long time."

"Longer than your lifetime," I commented.

She nodded. "But I thought you'd be scared. And if you weren't scared, or even if you were..." She looked down and then looked up at me from under her eyelashes. "You're a man. You're supposed to be entranced by me."

I said she was beautiful. Entrancingly so, and I could see how a lonely sailor might throw himself into the sea to swim to her, as she sat on a rock. I genuinely regretted that it was wasted on me.

"Well, lass..." And then I thought that she might not be younger than me, in spite of appearances. "Number one, I don't believe you're real, but my grasp on reality has been a bit shaky these last three months, so that's nothing new. Number two, I've seen a good deal worse than you in my nightmares. And number three, you are indeed a very beautiful, and undoubtedly charming, young lady, but even if I could work out *how* to ravish you, I wouldn't want to. I'm afraid you're rather wasted on me."

She pouted at me, an appealing gesture, and she obviously knew it. "Why?"

"Because, my dear, you're a mer*maid*."

She stared at me, and I saw the moment when she understood. Amusement blossomed in her face, and she threw back her head and laughed, a delighted and delightful pealing. Eventually she stopped. "Just my luck. I decide to sneak off and break the rules, and I come up with *you*."

I grinned back. "Sorry to disappoint you, pet." I decided that I liked this figment of my imagination. I was also less certain that that was what she was. I became even less certain when she made a grab for my groin. "Hey! Stop that!"

"Just checking. You *feel* interested." She patted me intimately and then looked puzzled. "You're different. You're interested, but soft."

Curiosity won the war with embarrassment. "Different to what?"

"One of my men. Take those clothes off."

I could see the headlines in my mind but did as she asked. She handled me firmly but carefully and quite clinically. "So mother wasn't exaggerating about landmen." She let go and calmly started asking me about sex. Not in a personal interest sort of way, mind. No, it was just that she was even more curious about how my body worked than I was about hers. And I was certainly curious about her. It turned out that she was half dolphin, not half fish; although the last time her people had made a public appearance nobody was bothering to make that distinction. Not *really* half dolphin, of course, but a mammal, and constructed at one end at least, like other sea-living mammals—my external genitalia were what had fooled her as to whether I was interested. And she had a full measure of curiosity from both the human and the dolphin side of her nature. We drifted from sex to other topics, neither of us noticing the time passing by.

Finally she noticed that the tide was receding, leaving her in danger of being left high and dry. "Will you be here tomorrow?" she asked plaintively, and I assured her that I would be, not voicing my doubts as to whether she would be.

She was and I was, and that's how I started spending several hours a day, whenever the tide was right, sitting in a rock pool talking to a mermaid. The pool wasn't totally enclosed at high tide, so Pearl could get in and out, but the rocks did provide shelter from the surf and somewhere for us to sit. Pearl was intelligent, insatiably curious, and utterly uninhibited. I delighted in her company, if not for the reasons she had expected. And then one day I arrived at the rock pool, and she said, "I want you to meet someone."

There was a sudden movement under the surface of the water, and then a splash, and I was looking at a man treading water. A merman, like Pearl to look at, but handsome where she was beautiful. This time the beauty wasn't wasted on me. Before I knew what I was doing, I was in the water, my mind dazzled by what I saw.

The shock of the cold water woke me. I'd stepped into the rock pool fully clothed, not thinking what I was doing, not thinking at all, and for the first time since I'd met Pearl, I was truly frightened. The splash as I went in had broken my eye contact with the merman, and I looked away. Then it was Pearl in my vision, and I remembered the legends, mermaids luring seamen to their doom. I was immune to Pearl, but only because Pearl wasn't what I wanted. Now the merfolk outnumbered me, and one of them was more than adequate bait even if the other wasn't. I tried to turn around and reach the rocks, fighting down panic, near to screaming when I felt a hand touch me.

I heard Pearl's voice, "I'm sorry, Mike, I didn't think…" Her hand helped me boost myself onto the rocks. I clambered out and turned around to look at Pearl—only at Pearl. She looked worried.

"It's just my brother, Mike. He wanted to meet you."

A simple enough explanation, and even if it wasn't, I thought I'd be safe on the rocks. I kept looking at Pearl, safe against her glamour at least. "Why?"

Another voice, a male version of Pearl's. "I wanted to know where Pearl was sneaking off to and made her tell me." Wistfully, he said, "She isn't the only one who wants to know about the landpeople."

There was a gurgle of laughter from Pearl. "And I'm not the only one who wants to find out what they're like to fuck."

I'd long since given up being surprised by her bluntness, but I still cringed with embarrassment for myself and her brother. Then it sunk in.

"Yes, dear," Pearl said. "Since you're not interested in me, I thought you might be interested in him. I didn't realize you'd be *that* interested, though. Maybe there is something to the tales about us being able to glamour landmen."

I risked a look at the merman. Lovely face, sleek black hair, fit but not over-muscled body, at least what I could see of it. Pensive expression at the moment; a shy man ready to turn tail. Literally, in this case.

Everything to press my buttons, so far as above the waist was concerned.

"I think"—I said carefully—"the only glamour concerned is what happens naturally when a man hasn't had any sex for a long time and then sees someone attractive."

Pearl's brother smiled tentatively, and Pearl, being Pearl, said, "Fancy fucking him, then?"

"Stop embarrassing us." And it was 'us', to judge by the poor man's expression. Well, I don't think I'd like *my* sister being quite that blunt in her matchmaking.

"Well?" she asked.

"Pearl, introduce us properly, and then *bugger off.*"

Pearl smirked. "His name's Malachite and buggering is what you two should be doing." Then she dived under with a cheeky flip of her tail. The last I saw of her was a dark shadow heading for the gap into the open sea.

I looked at Malachite. He was watching where his sister had gone. Then he turned back to me. "I don't trust her not to sneak back to watch."

"Funny, that. Neither do I."

We grinned at each other, and then I felt shy. So did Malachite by the look of things. Hardly any wonder in that; this wasn't quite your usual blind date for either of us. At least I had the advantage of nice long chats with Pearl; I had some idea about the differences in anatomy.

Come to think of it, Malachite had probably also had the advantage of nice long chats with Pearl.

That was why the little sneak had been feeling me up again yesterday. She'd claimed it was so that she could try to understand how land anatomy worked in comparison with her people so she could then explain it to me. Well, that *was* what she had been doing; she just hadn't bothered to mention that I wasn't the only one getting the benefit of her comparative anatomy studies.

I sighed. "I take it you've had the lecture on how the other half lives?"

He nodded.

"So how are we going to manage this?" The merpeople were mammals, air-breathers, but they were ocean-going air-breathers; they could manage far longer than I could. In the water wasn't the best idea. "The rocks are smooth enough." Hard, but smooth—no nasty edges to catch tender skin.

Malachite looked at the rock I was sitting on. It was a big, smooth rock, plenty of room for two people to lie on. There was a flicker of fear in his eyes. "No."

I'd seen fear like that before. One man wanting to play with bondage, the other not quite certain of his partner, willing to trust him with the use of his body, but not with control of it. I looked at the rock again. The merman was an ocean dweller, tail instead of legs. With the advantage the smooth flat surface would give me over him it might as well be a bondage rack.

"In the water," he suggested. "I'm strong enough to hold you up."

Strong enough to hold me up—or hold me down under the water. The legends came creeping back to haunt me, and I snapped "No" without even intending to.

Malachite looked startled and then resigned. "You don't trust me."

"Nor you me," I reminded him. "Not yet, anyway." Maybe later.

"Nets," he whispered.

Pearl had never said why her people had withdrawn centuries ago. They must have their legends too. Stalemate.

Then I thought of one place that was neutral territory. "The beach."

"Pardon?"

I looked towards the stretch of sand. Perfect. A calm day, the waves a gentle ripple. "On the beach, in the waves. We'll be on an equal footing there."

"Well, not quite," he said wryly, glancing down. Then he swam over to the rock and propped himself up on the edge, looking towards the sand. "Deep enough for me, shallow enough for you."

"Exactly."

He smiled up at me. "I'll meet you there." He pushed away from the rock edge and dived. I clambered to my feet, stripped off my sodden shorts and T-shirt, and ran for the shoreline. He beat me there, naturally. I waded out to meet him in the shallows where we both felt safe. I sat down, and he sat in my lap, smooth hide pressing against my cock. He kissed me, a clean fresh taste of sea. It had been a long time for me; I found myself groping for his cock, bewildered when I didn't find it, and then remembering, easing my hand into the narrow slit and stroking rigid flesh, easing it out where I could wrap my hand around it. He moaned into my mouth and shifted in my lap, trying to thrust into my hand. We tumbled over and had to let go of each other. We both came up spluttering and laughing.

I reached for him. "Shallower water, I think, and lie down." He nodded in agreement, and I towed him shoreward, to where the water was shallow enough for us to lie propped up on one arm, using the other hand to explore each other's bodies. Deep enough for him, shallow enough for me. He ran his hand down my side and over my legs, fascinated. I ran my hand down his side, feeling an equal fascination with his tail. It felt smooth and warm, not scaly at all. Back up and hands on cocks, different but good. My cock hanging free, swelling under his touch even in the cool water, his sheathed in that slit in his tail until I stroked it forth. More exploration, him fascinated by my arse, cupping one buttock. Me realizing that he was very different, dolphin-like with everything at the front; this man I could fuck face-to-face without any contortions. He saw my reaction and pulled me on top of him.

A frantic tug at his body, pulling him a little further up the slope, and then I could stop worrying about whether he could breathe, the water here shallow enough. I knelt straddling him, stroking one hand down the front of his tail, trying to find the right place. Then I had it and pushed a finger inside, testing that I wouldn't hurt him. He groaned with pleasure, not pain, eyes shut. Reassured, I laid myself down, fitting myself to him, into him. Exquisite tightness around me, his cock rubbing against my belly, muscular tail flexing between my legs. Then he tugged at my arse, pulling me all the way in, fire around my cock. One hand up to my head, pulling me down for a kiss.

And there we'd been worried about the surf making it difficult to breathe...

Arms around each other, me fucking him with my cock, him fucking me with his tongue, long slow strokes, then quicker strokes, and quicker, always in time with each other. Water lapping around us, a pleasant tickle against my skin, sun warm on my back, contrasting with cool splash. Hard and fast, and then he held still under me, and I gave him one last stroke, and he was clutching me to him, tight around me, tongue filling my mouth, and I came.

We clung together for a few seconds and then reluctantly pulled apart, sitting up to breathe. I had to support him with one arm; the water was too shallow to support his weight, and he couldn't get his tail quite right for balance. He leaned against me as we gasped for air. Then I managed to pull him into my lap where he could sit more comfortably, and we simply held each other for a while.

He broke the silence. "I must commend Pearl on her good taste."

"Thank you. I think."

He leaned close and nipped my earlobe. "Well, did you like it?"

"Should think that was obvious," I muttered.

"Enough for another go?"

"Good god, haven't you people ever heard of a refractory period?"

"Yes," he murmured into my ear, and by god, that was making me think about not having a refractory period. "We know about you landpeople and your little problem."

"Little!"

"I wasn't referring to your physical dimensions." He sat upright again and grinned smugly at me. "Those are more than adequate, thank you."

"And being able to get it up again?"

"Well, actually, we do have to wait a little while..."

"Good," I said, and kissed him long and hard. "I've got an idea. Back to the rock pool..." I pushed him out of my lap. He looked puzzled but went. "Let me pull you out where you won't be scraping your tail on the sand." I stood up and tugged him into deeper water where he could move comfortably. Deep enough for me to be wary of him, but then he'd come into water shallow enough for him to be wary of me. I waded back to shore. "Meet you there. I can walk it faster than I can swim."

Back at the rock pool, and I walked around it, checking the edge, Malachite watching me. As I'd thought, there was a spot where the rock dropped vertically into the pool, with a flat ledge out of the water that at this time in the tide was at the right height for me to lean on and the floor of the pool shallow enough for me to stand on and still breathe. I should have thought of this to begin with, but we'd both panicked in our separate ways and away from the rock pool altogether had probably been the best idea after all. I slipped into the water and called him over. He rested his hands on my shoulders, lifting himself up slightly. He was shorter than me, or at least the human half was, and had just enough depth of water not to be scraping the flukes of his tail on the bottom. I held his waist, giving him a little more support. "Now, I think we can both be happy here."

"Very much so." He grinned at me. "I think I'd like a closer look at the differences. Let go a minute."

I did so and he disappeared below the surface of the water where he started examining the differences, very closely indeed. Then his mouth closed around my cock, sucking first gently and then harder. Tongue moving over my cock and, ye gods and little fishes, water being sucked over the surface. I shuddered and grabbed his head, forcing him further on to me, and then guiltily let go, worrying about choking him, drowning him.

I needn't have worried. Like I said, ocean-living air-breathers...

I was close to coming when he finally surfaced; he was very close to collapsing. Instead, I grabbed him and pulled him close, kissing him again. He held me tightly, not just with his arms but also with that incredible tail twining around me. Then he let go. "Turn around."

I did so, reaching up to pull my arms onto the rock ledge, legs dangling free in the water. A trail of kisses down my spine, all the way down, and I spread my legs as much as I could. His tongue probed my hole, his hand cradling my balls, all with the gentle slap of water against my back. I rested my head on my arms and fought down the urge to thrust, letting him have his way, letting him sate his curiosity about my strange body.

He surfaced again, one hand on my shoulder for balance, the other at my arse, opening me up. "Tell me if it hurts. I've never done this before."

I was surprised at that, he seemed experienced, and then realized what he meant—that he'd never done it with someone of my shape before, rather than someone of my gender. "You're doing fine."

"Good." He bit gently at my shoulder. "Maybe we can manage it a bit more slowly this time."

He certainly managed his entry slowly; I was squirming in pleasure as he pressed in, urging him on, finally pleading with him to hurry up and shove it in. "No" was the simple, smug answer I got. Then he was seated in me, thrusting gently, and I was going crazy with desire. I thought it couldn't get any worse and then it did. He wrapped one hand around my cock and squeezed. He murmured in my ear, "It's quite a novelty being able to do it this way round." Of course, it would be for him; it might not even be physically possible to do it from behind with one of his own people. "I like being able to hold your cock while I fuck you," he said, and I realized that my new lover had a devastating line in dirty talk. And he wasn't even doing it on purpose, which only made it worse.

Somewhere about that point, my brain went on holiday, which would no doubt have pleased my doctor as she'd been nagging me on the subject for some weeks. I didn't think I'd tell her how I'd got laid, though. I simply floated there while a devastatingly attractive man told me how much he enjoyed playing with my cock, while demonstrating same and simultaneously fucking me senseless. I could feel myself building up to it and heard myself whimpering in pleasure, and then I was coming— one long glorious stream into the water.

I sagged onto the ledge, unable to do anything else to support myself. His weight sagged on top of me, rubbing me against the rock. The rock was smooth, but it wasn't *that* smooth. "Get off me a mo."

"Sorry."

He pulled away, which wasn't what I wanted. I wanted the body contact afterwards, just a bit more comfortably. I turned over reluctantly and swam over to the bit of rock I'd first suggested, grumbling internally all the way. It wasn't fair to have to exercise after taking a bit of exercise. Then I hauled myself out and flopped on the rock. "C'me here."

"Why?" he asked, all defensive now.

"Want a cuddle."

He looked at me warily and then swam over and leaned on the rock edge without getting out of the water. "That doesn't look very comfortable."

I hauled myself more or less upright, looked around, and discovered that my clothing was in reach. Wet, but softer than the rock. I folded up the shorts into a pillow for me and the T-shirt into a pillow for Malachite, put them both on the rock, and lay down again and closed my eyes. "I'm tired and I want a cuddle. This is normal post-coital behaviour in my species, even if it isn't in yours." Maybe it wasn't, at that.

I heard the sound of splashing and then felt a trickle of water run between me and the rock. I reached out and found a warm wet body to put my arm around. Warm wet *tailed* body. "Sorry, pet. Should have thought. This isn't very comfortable for you, is it? We'll have to think of something. I can't just lie there and float afterwards like you."

"You'll be here tomorrow then?"

Like sister, like brother. This one wasn't convinced either that I wouldn't decide it had all been a dream to forget as quickly as possible. "As soon as the tide's up. Ask your sister if you don't believe me."

"The only thing I'll be asking her is to stay away for a bit. Not that she will."

ACTUALLY, SHE DID, for a couple of days at least, and then she turned up all pleased with the success of her matchmaking. Nosy little cow. We eventually solved the problem of a bed to lie in afterwards. One of those inflatable mattresses floating in the rock pool did the trick—easy to get onto, easy to get off, for both of us. Of course, his horrible little sister is the same as any horrible little sister seeing her brother floating on an inflatable in a swimming pool and thinks it the world's greatest delight to come sneaking up underneath and tip it over. I can see I'm going to have to introduce her to some nice man to keep her quiet. Turnabout is only fair play, after all.

NAKED

BILL PULLED AT his bonds, testing. No, he couldn't get free now even if he wanted to, and the expression on Kevin's face was giving him some slight twinges of regret over that. He forced the fear down. He could trust Kevin.

Then Kevin showed him the razor. Not a safety razor that could do no more than nick his skin, but a folding knife. A cut-throat.

"You never said..."

Kevin grinned. "No. I didn't. You never asked." Then he set down the razor and picked up a brush and bowl. "I do like to do things *properly*. Otherwise why bother in the first place?"

Why indeed? Why was he doing this?

Then Kevin dragged the stiff bristles across his chest, across his nipples, and he knew why. Sensation trailing in the wake of the brush, hundreds of tiny pinpoints of touch packed together against his skin. Wetness after, plain water now, warm and then cooling on his skin. Kevin wetted him down with careful attention to detail and utter silence. He found the silence even more unnerving than the thought of the razor. Kevin was looking down at his task, eyes invisible, and Bill couldn't even read what little of Kevin's thoughts might be allowed to show on his face.

Then Kevin rubbed the brush against the soap with a sensual motion, an artist taking pride in his skill. A light lather collected on the brush and then transferred to him, nipples first again. Then a delicate swirl of sensation back and forth across his chest, cooler this time. The soap tickled slightly as it went on, leaving him with an urge to scratch. An urge he couldn't satisfy, not standing tied to this frame. "That tickles."

"Good." And Kevin went back to the table to set down the bowl and brush, leaving Bill thinking that the little bastard had deliberately set the table far away enough that he couldn't just turn to it. Bill had to stand and wait in anticipation. He also had an excellent view of Kevin's arse, all covered with Kevin's trousers. He'd only agreed to be tied. He hadn't expected Kevin to take the power game that little bit further by neglecting to undress or even change into something more appropriate. It would have been less disconcerting if Kevin had been wearing some sort of leather getup, instead of perfectly ordinary everyday clothing while *he* hung here with nothing more than a G-string to cover the bits that weren't to be shaved.

Kevin picked up the razor and returned. Not just a razor, but a strip of leather as well. He proceeded to strop the razor against the leather, slowly and methodically, stopping to turn the blade this way and that in the light as he checked the edge. "Don't worry, Bill, I'm careful with my toys. I don't want to cut you...by accident." He grinned again and dropped the leather on the floor. Two steps and Kevin was close enough to lay the blade against Bill's chest, a thin line of cold running down his sternum. Another chill line crept down his spine as he wondered just how much he did trust Kevin. Then the razor moved, whisking away the soap in a broad sweep above his nipples. Another below, and then Kevin laid the flat of the blade against one nipple and looked at him, devil's glint in his eye. "I suppose you'd like me to be careful with these?"

The shock of the cold blade against his nipple had deprived him of speech. It hadn't just been his imagination that it had felt like a line of ice when it had first touched him. Kevin must have had the damn thing in the fridge. Then he found his voice again. "You said..."

"No pain. And I keep my word, so I suppose I'd need to anaesthetise them first. I don't suppose a cold blade would be adequate to the task."

"No it bloody well wouldn't!" This was not what he'd expected at all. What he'd expected had been a lot of chat about Kevin having him where he wanted him, words to emphasise the power difference—to tell him that he was, however temporarily, Kevin's plaything. This...

Was frightening. Which was why Kevin was doing it. He hoped.

"Very well. Let me know if you change your mind." And with that, Kevin made a fast but delicate pass over his skin, the very tip of the blade whispering over one aureole. Before he'd quite decided if he'd imagined it, Kevin had moved onto his belly. Long strokes sweeping down, stopping at the very edge of the G-string, leaving Bill glad he'd worn one that went for relative modesty. He did his best to stand still, not to flinch; he couldn't blame Kevin if one of those long, controlled strokes met skin that had moved in the meantime.

Then it was done, and Kevin went back to exchange the razor for clean water and the brush. Water slopped onto him now, not delicately dabbed, rinsing away soap and hair and not, he was glad to see, blood. "You do have a delicate touch."

"That was the easy bit," Kevin said, patting him dry with a towel. His skin prickled oddly as the soft cloth moved across it. "Chests are mostly convex. Concave probably requires the safety razor, I'm afraid."

"The voice of experience?"

"Oh yes." Kevin leaned in close and kissed him, luxuriously. It was the first contact with Kevin since he'd been tied to this frame, and his cock loved it. His newly naked skin didn't know what to make of it, reacting to the strange sensation of Kevin's shirt pressed against it. The sensation was overwhelming, bizarre. Then Kevin pulled away, and he slumped against the ties, nerves jangling. He hadn't thought through what it would be like, that much skin with new-shaven sensitivity. He hadn't realised just how sensitive it would be. Now he knew why Kevin had suggested a trial run, rather than a whole body shave. He wasn't sure he could bear to be this bare all over.

Kevin moved back to him and did it all over again to his armpits. And then he stood in front of Bill with the cut-throat again, with the most wicked smile Bill had ever seen on his lips, and slid the tip of the razor beneath the string girdling Bill's hips.

"No!" he protested without conscious thought.

"Yes." And Kevin moved the blade, slightly, very slightly, but enough. The triangle of cloth fluttered to the ground, leaving Bill defenceless.

"I didn't agree to this!"

"You wanted it all when you first saw that magazine." Kevin's voice was coolly mocking.

"I just wanted..." What had he wanted when he'd found that magazine in Kevin's cupboard? "I wanted to understand why it turned you on."

"And why it turned *you* on?"

"Yes." He glared at Kevin. "I didn't think it included..."

"You should have thought. Or at least not tried to stuff the magazine down the back of the mattress when I walked in. I'd have been quite happy for you to read the last page or two."

'Read' wasn't really the appropriate word for something that consisted mostly of photos, of course. "Kevin, I'm not comfortable with this."

"My taste for D/s, or my specific tastes in D/s?"

"You having that razor near my balls."

Kevin looked at him, looked at the blade, and then went to the table and set it down. He came back to Bill and cupped his face. "Bill, I do know how to do this. I will be careful, and I won't hurt you. And I won't do it if you can't cope."

That last wasn't a dare; he could hear that in Kevin's voice. "All right," he said, voice shaking slightly.

Kevin kissed him again, very lightly. "Say if you want me to stop, and I will."

He could believe that; he could believe the trace of concern he'd seen in Kevin's expression. So he nodded and waited as Kevin collected the brush and water.

Kevin handled him carefully, lovingly, gently pushing his cock out of the way when necessary. The soap swirled through his pubic hair, making him horribly aware that the next thing to follow would be a sharp blade. Even the view of Kevin kneeling at his feet didn't help. Kevin might be kneeling, but Bill was the one tied in place.

Then the knife, and he closed his eyes. That was even worse; his imagination wasn't bounded by reality. At least it was just the top of his pubic hair to begin with, not so bad. He opened his eyes and forced himself to look down. Kevin was handling the knife with the same delicate precision he would any of his tools, and Bill relaxed ever so slightly. He concentrated on breathing evenly—it would help the incipient panic and make things easier for Kevin.

In the silence, he could hear a tiny scraping sound, the sound of sharp steel against his skin. His senses seemed heightened. Surely he shouldn't be able to hear something that quiet? The bare skin of his chest prickled in the slight air movement of the air conditioning. He could almost hear his own pulse.

Then Kevin started on his balls. Nothing new, the feel of a razor against that bit of skin—he'd shaved before for lovers who preferred it that way. But never like this: another's hand guiding the blade, his own hands tied. He shivered inside, trying not to shiver outside, trying to keep utterly still.

At last it was done and Kevin was rinsing him off. Then drying him off, and to his surprise, placing tender kisses along the exposed skin. This wasn't what he'd envisaged at all.

To his greater surprise, Kevin got up and fetched the bowl and brush back again. "Now what? I thought you said I shouldn't do the whole thing first time?"

"Just one more bit, Bill." Kevin walked behind him and spread his buttocks.

He jumped, as much as he could in the bonds. Somehow the idea of Kevin being where he couldn't see him was even worse than having to watch.

"I said I don't damage my toys, Bill." Slight edge of impatience there, which was more like the Kevin he'd thought he'd known. He held still.

More brushing of lather against his skin, making him want to squirm. He held still. The blade, not so cold now, not after the contact it had already had with his skin. He very definitely held still. Rinsed and dried, and he could twitch now, although Kevin slapped him lightly and told him to hold still.

Then unbelievable cold again, something poured between his buttocks. Something worked against the opening to his body. "*No, Kevin.*"

"You could let me hold a naked blade to your balls," a gentle whisper in his ear, "but you won't let me make love to you?"

He'd never let Kevin fuck him. But Kevin had never asked to make love to him.

He relaxed in his bonds, the last strength to resist gone. "Do what you want."

"Only if you want it too." Gentle. Implacable.

"You said you'd stop if I asked."

"I still will."

"All right, Kevin. Make love to me." *You have been, all evening, haven't you?*

"Thank you."

One finger eased its way in. He was sensitive, so sensitive, the light brush of Kevin's hand against shaven skin magnified so that he couldn't ignore it. Then Kevin's cock, and it felt huge between his buttocks. Not so huge once it went in, and somehow Kevin had the patience to stay still, let him adjust. Then Kevin put one arm around his waist, cupped the other hand over his cock and balls, and thrust against him.

Sensation overwhelmed him, filling him, surrounding him. His shaven skin was one enormous erogenous zone, all the nerve endings exposed. A slight twitch of Kevin's arm across his belly underlined the slide of Kevin's cock inside his body. The thrust into him forced him into Kevin's hand, his balls screaming their awareness of Kevin's fingertips.

Then Kevin slid an arm up his belly and grabbed his nipple, and he came in one long ecstatic stream, not caring whether Kevin followed.

He hung in his bonds, gasping for breath, barely noticing as Kevin slid out, noticing a little more as Kevin let go of him, exposing him to the air. He looked up as Kevin passed him, a small spark of curiosity left, and saw Kevin come back with the razor.

He wanted no more; he'd had as much as he could take. "Enough, Kevin."

"I know." Kevin lifted the razor. "Hold still."

One hand abruptly came free, and he realised what Kevin was about. Just in time, he shifted his weight, staggering a little but not falling as the other hand was freed.

Kevin folded the razor and let his hand fall to his side. "Do you understand now?" he asked quietly.

Oh yes, he understood. "Not all of it, but I don't think it's disgusting. I never did." He reached out and stroked one finger down Kevin's cheek. "Come to bed, love. We can talk about it in the morning."

ONE SIZE FITS ALL

GAVIN CHECKED THE corridor one last time and, satisfied that it was clear, slipped inside the bedroom. It would never do if Hugh caught him—Hugh had a strong sense of privacy, to the point of preferring to go to Gavin's place rather than his own. But since he'd given Gavin a key and agreed to meet here tonight...

Yes, Hugh did keep his underwear in the obvious place. Black, black, black—oh, there's a surprise, grey—black, deep blue—good god, the man did own something that wasn't neutral colours—black...

All very severe. Just as bad as everything Hugh had worn so far when calling on him of an evening. The man was a delight in bed but had *no* idea of underwear as a turn-on rather than as something to keep warm with. He'd hoped Hugh might have something a bit more entertaining tucked away, but no, it was all the same severe, dark stuff. The high proportion of silk to cotton was all very well, but couldn't it be silk for the sake of silk, rather than because it was warm and comfortable?

That wasn't silk.

He scrabbled it out from under the pile of socks. Given what it was, it had probably been hidden under there deliberately. Black again, but this time leather. He sniffed at it. Clean, but definitely *used* leather. Leather with a slight overlay of Hugh.

Very nice. He tried to picture Hugh wearing it—and nothing else. Even nicer. Why hadn't Hugh worn it with him? Embarrassed? Maybe he was; after all, the idea of buttoned-up Hugh wearing something like this was a bit...well, a bit of a shock. Two black leather triangles held together by a strategically placed metal ring and a couple of buckled straps, one-size-fits-all. Not really the sort of thing anyone expected Hugh to wear. Of course, most people didn't notice that reserved, quiet Hugh even had a sex drive—Gavin had bagged him by the simple expedient of being the first in their social group to notice that he did.

Just how one-size-fits-all was this thing, anyway?

The idea wouldn't go away. There was something very appealing about the idea of wearing leather that had last held Hugh in an intimate clasp. He'd only come in here to rummage around for something to have waiting for Hugh, but this wasn't what he'd expected to find. Hugh as a secret leather fetishist was quite a turn-on. Maybe the silk wasn't just for warmth and comfort.

It was no good; he couldn't resist. He fiddled with the straps, letting them out until they seemed about the right fit, stripped quickly, and pulled it on. Not quite right on the straps, so he let them out a little bit more. That seemed to fit around the waist, but it was still a bit tight around the front. He went over to the mirror so that he could see what he was doing. His cock was poking out of the top of the triangle, and his balls were peeking around the sides. No wonder he wasn't comfortable. He tried adjusting things.

One ball in, and the other popped out completely. Maybe it was still too tight. He loosened the straps a little more and carefully tucked his balls in, one in each hand so that one didn't push the other out. The leather slipped down, and his cock waved merrily from the top. Damn. Tighten the straps a little, some fumbling to get all three bits under control, cock in and thumbs on it to keep it down, fingers spread to tuck his balls in. There. That looked rather nice. For about two seconds, and then he was bursting out all over again. How did Hugh manage this? He himself might be on the well-built side, but Hugh wasn't exactly underendowed, given their relative body sizes.

"You're supposed to put it on before you reach maximum size."

He jumped, which wasn't really the wisest thing to do when he had one hand tucked inside a recalcitrant piece of leather. "Hugh! I wasn't expecting you to get home this early."

"Obviously. Why were you looking through my underwear?"

He could feel himself flushing. Ridiculous, really. What was wrong with wanting your new lover to try a little harder in the sexy underwear department? "It's not that I don't appreciate you, it's just that—" *How could he put this?* "—well, I like sexy underwear. I thought you might have something more interesting that I could get you to wear."

Hugh grinned sardonically. "And you thought you'd try it on for size."

Well, yes, he could see it from Hugh's point of view. "I was curious."

Hugh looked him up and down. "It seems to suit you."

Now what was *that* supposed to mean?

Hugh walked over to him and deftly tucked him in.

"How did you manage that?" *Lots of practice?*

"As I said, you're supposed to put it on before reaching maximum size." Hugh ran a hand over the leather. "You seem to have wilted slightly."

"Keep that up, and that won't be a problem."

"Oh, good." Hugh squeezed gently. "I think I'd like to see you wearing it properly."

"Hugh." He wondered how to broach a somewhat delicate subject. "How long have you had this?"

"Longer than I've had you."

"*Why* did you have it?"

Hugh smiled secretively but gave no other answer.

He made to undo one of the buckles but was stopped by Hugh holding his wrist. "I said I want to see you wearing it properly." Hugh's other hand was on the leather, a firm caress, cradling his cock and balls. He was starting to swell again, and not just because of the touch. He thrust forward against Hugh's hand. Hugh squeezed him through the supple leather, and he thrust again. There was a thrill to standing here wearing nothing but a ridiculous scrap of leather while his fully clothed lover brought him to readiness. One hand over his cock, the other now tracing around his nipples.

Hugh let go and stepped back. "*Much* better."

He looked in the mirror. Hard swell of cock against leather, but this time confined—the leather tight against him, squeezing him. Too long and it would be painful, but for now it was erotic—both to feel and to see.

Hugh stood behind him, and put both hands on his buttocks, massaging them through the leather. "Yes, you look very nice. Better than I do."

The mental image of Hugh standing in front of this mirror, looking at himself, nearly proved the undoing of the leather knickers.

The hands on his arse were working inwards now, and then he felt a sharp chill. The metal ring pressed against his bare flesh. Then something else—something much warmer—Hugh's finger.

He looked at Hugh in the mirror. They hadn't done this yet; they'd been too busy experimenting with other ways of fitting their bodies together. Hugh said nothing aloud; he could ignore it if he wanted. But the question was there in Hugh's eyes.

Did he want to do this?

Yes.

He pushed back, and the tip of Hugh's finger slid inside him. Hugh smiled at him and then kissed the back of his neck. Hands running up his back, caressing his shoulders, and then Hugh said, "Make me ready."

He turned around, dropping to his knees. He pushed up Hugh's jumper so that he could reach the fastening of his trousers, made his way inside, and drew out Hugh's cock. Not that Hugh looked as if he needed much work to make him ready. Cock full and heavy, resting plumply in his hand. He kissed the tip and then bent to his task, licking and sucking. Not to make Hugh come, not this time, but to make him hard and wet, wet enough to slip smoothly inside him. He trembled slightly at the thought and heard Hugh gasp.

Like that, do you? He leaned forward, taking as much as possible, and sucked hard and then slid off. Hugh moaned, hands twisting in Gavin's hair. He pulled Hugh's trousers down a little—enough that he could nuzzle lower down, flicking his tongue over Hugh's balls.

"Enough, Gavin!" Hugh's voice was ragged.

He obeyed, sitting back on his heels and looking up at Hugh.

"Good. Stay there."

This was definitely turning interesting. He watched as Hugh efficiently stripped, enjoying the view of the compact body that felt so good against his own. Then Hugh went to a drawer, pulling out a small tube. It looked to be full.

Have you been keeping that for me?

Hugh turned back to him. "Kneel on the bed." Definitely a command, but the tone gentle. He obeyed, placing himself with his arse facing Hugh.

"Have you done this before?" Hugh asked.

He briefly debated giving Hugh a thrill by saying no but decided that Hugh would be annoyed, or hurt, to discover later that it was a lie. "Yes. But not often."

"Then we will need this."

He wasn't so certain about that, but if he insisted on trying without and failed, Hugh would *definitely* be annoyed. He kept quiet and waited. A wet finger at his hole, easing in. Nice touch there—Hugh had had the courtesy to warm the lube first. Inside, and deeper in, spreading the wetness within him.

"Is that enough, or do you want more?"

He was out of practice, and Hugh was well built, but the idea of being stretched by Hugh's cock... "I'll be fine."

"Then turn over."

He did so, surprised. He'd thought Hugh was heading into something a bit rougher, but apparently Hugh intended to take advantage of the bed being at a comfortable height for one man standing next to it and another lying on it. He looked up at Hugh's face. Hugh was not looking down at his, but somewhere further down his body. And clearly liking what he saw. One hand over the bulge in the leather. One word. "Mine."

"Yours," he agreed.

"You come when I tell you that you can."

"Yes." So there was something to the leather, after all.

Hand trailing over his cock, down to his thigh. Hugh's other hand on the other thigh, both sliding around underneath to give support. "I want you at the edge of the bed."

He shuffled forward so that he was right on the edge and then lifted his legs, settling them over Hugh's shoulders for support. He felt exposed and vulnerable, and he didn't give a damn. Not when Hugh *looked* exposed and vulnerable, emotion playing over his face. *Gentlest top I ever saw.*

Hugh caressed him, looking into his eyes now. They held still for a few seconds, and then Hugh slid one hand off Gavin and onto his own cock, guiding it as he thrust forward.

It was tight, but he looked up at Hugh, watching as Hugh caught the edge of his lip with a tooth, concentrating. A slight twinge, and then he was slowly filled up, pressure within and without. Hugh right up against him, checking his reaction, and then pulling out, only to push in again, blissful movement inside him. The leather restraint was a delightful torment, squeezing him hard, dragging against him slightly as Hugh moved, cold metal ring rapidly warming as it was pushed against him. The sharp contrast between cold-hard metal and warm-hard Hugh thrilled him inside.

Faster and harder, and he wanted to come now, excited as much by the sight as the feel of Hugh, and then remembering that the leather he was wearing had first been worn by Hugh, and it was keeping him from coming, and he wanted to come.

He only realised that he was trying to slip his hand inside the leather when Hugh pulled it out. "Wait for permission."

And, of course, that only made him want it even harder.

No gentleness in Hugh now, thrusting deep, his face wild. Then Hugh stopped, held still, before reaching a hand down to Gavin's hip.

Movement, scraping against his skin, and then he realised what was happening: Hugh was undoing a buckle. None too soon; he wanted it desperately now. Blessed release of pressure just as Hugh commanded, "Come," and he did come, grabbing Hugh's hand, holding tightly as he rode the waves of pleasure. Thinking somewhere in the middle of it all that now the leather would smell of both of them, and how the hell did Hugh clean it anyway?

SOMETIME LATER, he realised that he felt empty inside. Hugh had pulled out and was now undoing the other buckle—with shaking fingers, Gavin was pleased to note. His legs were still over Hugh's shoulders. He tried to ease them down, realised he couldn't—he was shaking as well.

Hugh left the buckle alone. "Let me do it."

Between them, they managed to get disentangled. He turned around to lie full length on the bed, and Hugh crawled on top of him, kneeling over him to tackle the buckle. The leather fell away. Hugh moved to one side. "Spread your legs."

"Thought I'd already done that." He grinned, and Hugh grinned back. Then he obliged, and Hugh obliged him by pulling out the leather. It was an interesting sensation, dragged out from under his backside. Then Hugh dropped it unceremoniously over the side of the bed and lay down next to him.

He decided it was his turn to be cuddled. They'd been fairly even-handed until now in the actual sex, but somehow he'd always ended up holding Hugh afterwards. This time he was going to be the one held in a comforting embrace. He pillowed his head on Hugh's shoulder and draped an arm across his chest. To his surprise, Hugh didn't object and merely said, "Lift your head for a second."

He did so, and Hugh slid an arm under his neck. As he settled down again, Hugh slid the arm around his shoulders, holding him. It was very pleasant. He said so.

Hugh said nothing in reply and merely lifted the other hand to stroke his head. Curiouser and curiouser.

They dozed for a while, enjoying the afterglow. Eventually Hugh nudged him. "I'm cold."

As usual... "Then get the duvet."

Harder nudge. "I can't until you get off me."

Oh, well, it had been too good to last... He let go of Hugh and said, "We really need to get you one with about twice the filling on one side of the bed as on the other."

"Tomorrow."

No complaints about invasion of Hugh's personal space? They were definitely doing better.

Hugh sat up and dragged up the covers. Then Hugh lay down again and put an arm around him.

Still cuddling him. Well, if Hugh was in that good a mood, he'd take advantage of it. "Why did you have those leather knickers?"

Sleepy smile in response. "Why did you try them on?"

"I liked the idea of you having worn them before me."

"Mmm."

He thought about that. "You said you'd had them longer than you'd had me."

"Mmm."

"You got them for me, even before you had me?"

"I got them because I thought I wouldn't have you."

That was certainly a roundabout way of saying whatever it was that Hugh was saying. He stroked Hugh's face. "Do you find me that intimidating?"

Hugh looked down. "Never thought you'd let me..."

So much for his ability to read people. It had never occurred to him that that might be why Hugh hadn't suggested fucking. Poor little sod had simply assumed that he'd end up on the bottom. "Hugh, I happen to like letting someone else take charge in bed." He watched Hugh's face. "You haven't much experience with leather, have you?"

Hugh still didn't look at him, but there was a small quirk of his mouth. "Only in my imagination."

"Obviously a very *vivid* imagination."

"Just how far off was it?"

"How the hell would I know? Underwear's *my* fetish."

Hugh laughed out loud and finally looked him in the eye. "And what about that not being on the bottom very often, if you like someone else taking charge?"

"Well, there's being on the bottom, and then there's *being* the bottom." He took hold of Hugh's hand, wrapping it around his cock. "For some reason, I find that partners take one look at that and want to tie me down so that they can make merciless use of it."

Hugh squeezed Gavin's cock and licked his lips. "I can't imagine why. Perhaps I should try it to find out."

He grabbed Hugh around the waist and rolled on his back so that Hugh was lying on top of him. "Perhaps you should. But will you *please* wear something sexy?"

Hugh grinned wickedly at him. "You didn't go all the way to the back of my sock drawer, did you? Let me up."

He did so and watched as Hugh sashayed his way over to the drawer in question. One sultry look over his shoulder, and he said, "It wasn't just leatherwear in that shop."

No, it wasn't. Silk again, but this time heavy white satin. Elasticated, so that a man could slip a hand, or a cock, inside. And a small bolt of cloth. "I thought I could get some more made, but there's enough here for ties instead," Hugh said as he came back to the bed.

Gavin ran a hand over the latest sample of silk. Oh yes, much more to his taste. "So where are we putting the eyebolts we're buying tomorrow? Your place or mine?"

"Both."

THE FRAUDSTER

TAKING DAVID MARR on was a risk. He was out on licence from a prison sentence. It was a risk I was willing to take, since he was not a man convicted of a violent crime, but a fraudster. But he'd had violence done to him while he'd been in prison—his probation officer warned me about that.

"Don't touch him or startle him," she'd said. "He's not a violent man, but he was assaulted in prison, and he's jumpy."

"And determined to go straight." Which was why I wanted him in spite of his criminal record. I wanted him *because* of his criminal record. I wanted a man capable of tracing the sort of crime he'd committed, and he'd been a very successful crook. He'd been caught by sheer bad luck.

"It might be more accurate to say he's determined never to go back inside," his probation officer said.

"You're very cynical."

She sighed. "No, experienced. Although I think David will behave as long as he thinks he's better off doing so. There's no malice to him, just too much curiosity and not enough common sense. Thanks for taking him on."

"I need someone with his skills. And someone who thinks like a computer crook."

I SAID THE same thing to him the next week when he asked me why a forensic accountant wanted to take on someone like him. "I know about computers, but I'm the mainframe generation, and I only ever used them as tools. I need someone who understands desktops. And the desktop generation of crackers."

"Set a thief to catch a thief," he said.

"Exactly. Are you willing to work with me?"

He grimaced. "I don't have much choice, do I?" he said softly. "Early release is dependent on showing that I'm a good citizen now. But how many people will employ me?"

I looked him over. "At least you look respectable—that will help." Middle class. Average height, average build, average looks. Nice-looking, but not out of the ordinary. Medium-brown hair with a touch of auburn highlighting. Medium-brown eyes. Medium everything, really, which would be an advantage. Nobody would take a blind bit of notice of him, which would be useful when working on-site.

"Does that matter to you?" he asked.

I nodded. "I know that people aren't always as respectable as they look. It's my job to dig out the financial secrets of terribly respectable people, after all. But you'll be of more use to me if people don't take one look at you and call security."

"Why me?"

"Because you're an honest crook," I said. David Marr had turned Queen's evidence, and he'd kept his side of the bargain. He'd turned in his accomplices and testified against them in exchange for a lighter sentence—and he'd only made that bargain after he'd been shown that they'd done the dirty on him, left him as scapegoat.

He thought that one over and then said, "When do I start?"

"Now."

"I still need to arrange accommodation..."

I'd already discussed that with the probation officer. My offices occupied the ground floor of a converted Victorian terrace house, and I'd found it convenient to buy the freehold of the whole house and live over the shop. "There are spare bedrooms in the flat upstairs. You can have one of them for a bit." He should have been told that, but maybe he didn't think he could afford it. "I'll dock it out of your salary, so it'll give you a bit of breathing space before you have to find somewhere that wants money up front."

He smiled slightly, transforming his face. No, he wasn't just nice-looking—he was one of those men who are beautiful only when you catch them a certain way. I could see why he'd had trouble in prison, over and above what any middle-class, educated man might face. "The better to keep an eye on me?" he asked.

"Convenience, but your probation officer seemed to like the idea."

He nodded, then stood up and walked over to the desk. My desk, as it happened. He flicked the mouse to bring the monitor up from power save.

Too late, it occurred to me that he might not like my choice of monitor wallpaper.

He stared at the picture from the collection I'd downloaded from the gay erotica newsgroup. It didn't leave anything at all to the imagination, and of course, this morning's selection had to be the one featuring hot and heavy anal action.

Mortified, I went over and turned the monitor off. "I'm sorry. I didn't think." I looked at him. He'd turned pale. I pulled out the desk chair. "Here, sit down."

He sat down and then looked at me, his mouth twisted. "Do you normally leave that running where your clients can see it?"

"Not that particular picture, no. But the less in-your-face ones are useful for checking whether a client's going to be a problem about thinking gays must be a security risk." I patted him on the shoulder. "I should have got rid of it before you arrived, but it was still running from last night, and I forgot."

He stared at my hand on his shoulder as if I'd dropped something repellent there.

I backed off, holding my hands up. "Sorry. I know you've got a problem with gays. If you want to back out of this arrangement, I'll talk to your probation officer. No hard feelings."

"I don't have a problem with gays. I have a problem with rapists." His attitude softened slightly. "It's not you. It's anyone." Then he said, "At least you're not going to insist that you can't be gay because you're on top."

Oh hell. I went and got the other desk chair, rolling it around so I could sit in front of him. If I loomed over him, it wouldn't help matters. I reached out for his hand and patted it, trying to make it nonaggressive. His hand was icy; he'd been badly shocked. "Let's have this out now. Yes, I'm gay. Yes, I think you're attractive. No, I don't regard my assistant as one of the perks of the job. And I certainly don't think that you must be gay because someone forced you." He blinked at that; I'd scored a hit. Well, it was fairly obvious what the corollary was to 'I'm on top'. "Now, I don't think it will all be all right with a nice cup of tea, but I think we may as well have one. It will give you a chance to calm down."

He sighed and said, "Thank you for being so understanding. Yes, I would like a cup of tea."

He followed me through to the kitchen. There was a proper kitchen upstairs in the flat, but the office suite had a small kitchen as well. He watched carefully as I made the tea, obviously memorising where things were. I handed him his mug and noticed that he didn't flinch when our hands touched. Good.

He did wait for me to go through the door first. I asked, "Still nervous about having people behind you?"

"Not just for that reason. Is that why you were willing to take on a convict? You know what it's like to be on the outside of society?"

I hadn't actually thought of it that way. "Not consciously. I suppose I'm less inclined to go by the surface; I know people aren't always what they seem. But I know that from my work, as well as my recreation."

"Tell me more about your work."

So I did. He was an eager listener—I thought he was genuinely interested in what I had to say. After an hour, I said, "Most people don't find accountancy so interesting."

"What you do isn't so dissimilar to a programming problem. You're the man who does the debugging."

Yes, he was the one I needed. "That's a good way to look at it. Not just the debugging, but tracking down malicious code. Speaking of which..." I got up and rummaged in my desk drawer for the work I wanted to start him on. I handed him the laptop. "First job. Go through that and look for anything useful."

He looked at the laptop and then at me. "You're trusting."

"No I'm not. You're the second opinion."

He nodded and took the laptop to his desk. He spent the rest of the day with it, eating lunch at his desk. I had to drag him away to eat dinner.

He ate like a starving man at first and then forced himself to slow down and savour it. "It's good."

"It's only a Chinese takeaway." A good one, from a decent restaurant nearby, but still only a takeaway. I'd phoned for a delivery since I didn't want to leave him alone in the house. Not just protective of my possessions—protective of him. I wasn't sure how he'd get on with being left on his own while I went out to fetch something.

"It's been a year."

A year that had left its marks on him. I looked him over. He looked tired. "Have an early night. It's your first day. Don't push yourself too hard."

"Are you going to tuck me up in bed?" Not quite a joke.

"This is an old house; it was built when they expected to lock internal doors. And the keys here work from both sides of the door. Lock yourself in if you'll feel safer that way."

He stared at me. "Why are you being so decent to me?"

"I'm an accountant." I shrugged. "I see worse than you every week. You were just stupid enough to get caught, and naive enough not to have stolen enough to qualify as rich and eccentric and one of the boys—just a misunderstanding, ho ho."

He smiled at that. A proper smile, and it took my breath away. I hid my reaction; he didn't need to have me lusting after him to add to his worries. "You're very cynical," he said.

"I've seen enough crooks in my time. I've helped put a few behind bars, but not enough of them. What you did was wrong. You were stealing from people, no matter how your friends tried to justify it as stealing from a corporation. But you didn't steal anyone's life savings and call it honest business."

"Thanks for not preaching at me." He looked at me from under his eyelashes. "Thanks for everything."

Long, thick eyelashes. Damn him. I was having a hard time remembering that this was someone I shouldn't make a pass at, no matter how polite. Quite apart from whether he wanted sex with anyone at all, he couldn't give free consent. Not when he thought that he was dependent on my good will for his continued freedom. "Remember, I'm doing this for my own benefit," I reminded him.

He nodded. "I'm not just doing it because I have to. It's interesting."

"Interesting enough to stop you getting so bored you start pissing with the system just to see if you can?"

"I was a fool, wasn't I?"

He sounded so bitter. It must have hurt to find he'd been played for a fool by the people who'd tempted him into taking it further than curiosity. "Yes. But you're not the first, and you're not the last, and you have another chance. Learn your lesson. You paid a high enough price for it."

"Now you are preaching."

"I know. But I think you're going to be useful, and I want you in a fit state to work for me. If that means a pep talk to remind you that it's worth hanging on, I'll preach." I stood up. "Want a drink?" I hadn't wanted to offer him anything until he'd had something to eat—he'd been in an open prison for most of his sentence, but I wasn't sure if they were allowed alcohol, and I didn't want him drinking on an empty stomach.

"Not until I've finished. But thanks."

Sensible man. I put the kettle on instead, not wanting to drink in front of him. We chatted about the work, avoiding the topic of his prison sentence. After dinner I offered him a small brandy, but he refused that as well.

"I'll probably have nightmares. I'd better be able to wake up if I do." He glanced at the bookcase. "May I borrow something to read?"

"Help yourself."

He picked out a book and said goodnight, leaving me alone. Leaving me wondering exactly what I'd got myself into. It might have been a mistake to offer him lodgings, but I could hardly throw him out now. I'd just have to think pure thoughts for a while.

I MANAGED TO think mostly pure thoughts for the rest of the week. He worked hard and got some useful results within the first few days. Too hard for his own good, I thought, for he went to bed early every night. I heard him whimpering in the middle of the night once, when I went to bed late, but didn't risk going in to him. I didn't think he'd thank me for it.

How right I was I didn't find out until Friday night.

We'd finished early; I'd happened to get the current case finished mid-afternoon. He'd finished his work around four, and I wouldn't let him start anything new. "Time you went for a walk. You haven't been out of this house since you arrived."

I was surprised he hadn't made the most of his new freedom. It became obvious as we walked along the street that he simply hadn't felt able to cope, although he said nothing about it. Just stayed close to me, even reaching for me once when someone jostled him. I put an arm around him, steadied him. "All right?"

He nodded. "It's a bit much. God knows how the long-termers cope when they get out."

Well, if he was willing to talk about it... "I thought you had day release?"

"Only to the village. This is more crowded. All these strangers..."

"Say if you can't handle it, and we'll go home."

"I'll manage. What are we having for dinner tonight?"

"I was planning on being extremely unhealthy and indulging in fish and chips."

His eyes lit up at that. "Real fish and chips?"

"Fried on the spot. Soaked in vinegar and wrapped in newspaper."

For that, he was willing to walk around window-shopping until dinner time. We queued for our fish supper and walked home, clutching our hot parcels. I enjoyed mine all the more for seeing how much he enjoyed his, and it wasn't just from watching him sucking his fingers to get the last of the flavour. No washing up tonight—just dump the paper in the bin, and wash our hands.

This time, he did accept a small glass of brandy from me, smiling up at me as I handed it to him. "I think I can risk it, if we're not working tomorrow."

"I work weekends when I have to, but not if I can help it." I sat down next to him on the sofa. "Have you thought about what to do with your weekend?"

"Not really. I thought maybe go for a walk, but I'll leave that until Sunday, when it's quieter."

"Nobody you want to visit?"

"Nobody who'd want me to." He took a sip of brandy and then said, "No, that's not fair. But it would mean more travelling than I want to do just yet. Better to leave it a week or two." He leaned back against the sofa, cradling the brandy balloon in his hand. "It's a bit odd, this. You're not just my boss, you're my landlord. And my nursemaid."

"I don't mind the company." I didn't. I can be picky that way; it's not everyone I'd want underfoot twenty-four hours a day. But he wasn't underfoot, and that was what made the difference. I was intensely aware of his presence for more than one reason, but he wasn't intrusive. "Anything you want to watch on telly?"

"Gardening programme?"

"Fine by me."

We settled down to watch BBC2 for the evening. Somewhere along the way he fell asleep, and I carefully took the glass from him and took it out to the kitchen. When I got back and sat on the sofa, he settled against me. I put my arm around him, trying to ease him into a comfortable position, and he ended up with his head pillowed on my shoulder.

Poor little sod. Too tired to even wake up. I twisted round a little to hold him with both arms and kissed the top of his head without thinking.

And that was when he woke up.

He jerked upright, fury twisting his face. "Get off me!"

Before I could let go of him, he'd smashed an elbow into my ribs and shoved me away from him. I scrambled away but lost my balance, falling to the floor. He landed on top of me, screaming obscenities, ripping at my clothes.

"It'll be the other way around this time! I don't go underneath just because I'm queer!"

"David! It's me! You're safe!" My guts had turned to water; I was going to disgrace myself in a minute. What had I let into my home, and would I even live to regret it?

"Bastard!" Heavy blow to my back, and then his weight lifted off me. I seized the chance to roll over, ready to kick him in the balls if I had to.

His face was contorted with rage, and he was readying a punch. And then something seemed to happen inside him—the demon let go. His hand relaxed, and the anger drained away, leaving shock behind. Then terror.

I scrambled to my knees, ready to get to my feet and run if necessary. I didn't think it would be.

He was swaying slightly, his face chalk-white, obviously in shock. He stared at me. Finally he whispered, "I'm sorry, Brendan."

"So you damn well should be." It hurt to talk; I could still feel where he'd thumped me in the ribs. I considered levering myself back onto the sofa and then decided it was easier just to sit on the floor and lean back against it. "What the hell was all that about?"

"You were..." he trailed off.

"I damn well was not." If he hadn't attacked me, I'd have been feeling guilty about the kiss, but his response was out of all proportion. "You...cuddled up to...me... And you might have been asleep when you did that, but you were awake when you started trying to tear my clothes off." Only then did I think about what he'd actually said. *Just because I'm queer.*

"I wasn't awake," he said, sounding miserable. "Not at first. Then I woke up and realised what I was doing. That I was fighting with you, only you were...you..."

"Sleepwalking." It made sense, fitted with the way he'd behaved. He'd looked...as if he'd woken from a nightmare, only he'd been dreaming with his eyes awake and his body acting out the dream.

"Do you want me to leave?"

"No." It wasn't his fault. I wasn't throwing him out at this time of night. "But I think it would be sensible to lock the door tonight."

He nodded. "You'd better lock it from the outside. If I'm capable of sleepwalking, I'm quite capable of unlocking the door without realising it."

"I was going to lock my door. From the inside. Unless you want to take a bucket into your room."

He relaxed, ever so slightly. "I'd rather not be locked in."

"I'm still taking the key to the front door. I don't want you wandering the streets in that state."

"And I can't afford to get arrested." He rubbed at his face and then looked at me. "Are you all right?"

"No. But I will be. Are you?"

He slumped back against the sofa, eyes closed. "No. But I will be. I hope."

He was still white and shaking very slightly. I felt sorry for him, in spite of my sore chest. I shuffled a bit closer and said, "David, I'm going to hold you."

No reaction. I wasn't sure whether that was good or bad, but put my arms around him anyway. He stiffened and then relaxed into my arms, laying his head on my shoulder once again.

"It's all right; you're safe here," I soothed.

"I know."

"What you said, when you were dreaming... Are you gay?"

Silence for a moment. "Bi."

"And someone realised and decided that made you a legitimate target."

"More or less."

"Look, I'm not trying to seduce you. I just think you need someone to hold you for a bit, no strings attached." I stroked his back, hoping he'd take it for what it was—comfort. "Let me know when you've had enough."

He actually put an arm around me then and held on. We stayed like that for a few minutes, and then I eased him off me. I'd stopped being angry with him and was starting to feel more than just protective, and he didn't need that.

He sat up and leaned back against the sofa. He still looked pale, but at least he wasn't scared any more. I'd done the sleepwalking thing a few times, but only ever found myself sitting in the kitchen or wandering around the bedroom. To wake up and find that you were assaulting your employer must be a fairly horrifying experience, even if you weren't at risk of going back to jail.

"Will you manage now?" I asked.

He actually smiled a little. "It's not that bad, honestly. I'd more or less got over it; I just have the occasional bad night. I'm sorry you got caught up in it."

"You're sure?"

"It was only the first week. After that, the police managed to get me moved somewhere safer. They were pretty pissed off about what happened to me, since they'd promised to look after me. Makes it harder to get the next potential witness to turn." He shrugged. "I've had a year to get over it."

I hadn't been told about that. The probation officer had told me he'd been assaulted, and I'd assumed that was a euphemism for raped, especially after his reaction the first day, but I'd not been given any of the details. He spoke of it casually now, but it was clear that it had had a lasting impact on him. Well, if denial was his way of living with it, I wasn't going to interfere.

He stood up and offered me a hand. I took it. I'm older than him, never mind having been knocked about by him, so the help up was welcome. Then I asked, "Do you want to go to bed just yet?"

"No. I want to be sure I won't go straight back into a nightmare."

"BBC2?"

He sat on the sofa, and I sat next to him. It was a repeat, as usual, but as usual, the repeats were better than the new stuff. Or more comforting at any rate. I slid my arm around his shoulders. He glanced at me before settling back, saying, "It's all right when I'm awake."

"Good."

"It's nice to be able to enjoy it without worrying that you're going to jump on me."

Not a warning off, but an honest statement. He'd accepted that he could trust me not to jump on him.

It might be a long, slow courtship, but I had the time and patience. I'd quite enjoy being allowed to take it slowly, instead of it being assumed that if I wasn't immediately all over him, I wasn't interested.

I WAS WOKEN the next morning by a light knock on my bedroom door. I went over to unlock it and found David holding a mug of tea in each hand.

"What time is it?"

"Nine. Wasn't sure if you liked to sleep in late at weekends."

I took mine and went back to bed to drink it. I'd overslept a little, but it was the weekend, and I didn't need to leap out of bed. He followed me in and sat on the edge of the bed. Well, we seemed to be making progress. "Would you like a cuddle?"

He smiled at me. "Yes, I would." He shifted along the bed, swung his legs up, and leaned back against the headboard. I put an arm around him, and we sat sipping our tea in perfect decorum.

"What would you like to do today?" I asked after a while.

"I suppose I should do something about picking up my life again." He sighed. "I do have people I should see, and sooner or later, I'm going to have to do something about finding somewhere to live."

"You don't have to move out, you know. I only offered temporary accommodation because I didn't know whether I wanted to offer long-term accommodation." I leaned over him and set my mug down on the bedside table. "And this"—I squeezed his shoulders—"isn't what makes the difference. It's a matter of whether I can live with you, not whether I'm shagging you."

"Passed the test, have I?" he asked rather wryly.

"You don't get in the way; you don't make a mess; you don't expect me to entertain you; and you don't do any of the other things that have previously caused me to give up on the idea of saving money by sharing. I wouldn't have chucked you out until you'd had a chance to get yourself together, but I wouldn't be offering a long-term option if I didn't think we could live together without you driving me up the wall."

"That sounds like the voice of experience."

"Oh, it is." I sighed, thinking about the experience. "I try it about once a year. Unfortunately, I get just enough of the good ones, who then find reasons to move on, that I'll risk the bad ones."

"Surely you don't need the money."

After a week working for me, it would have been surprising if he hadn't picked that up. The fact that I could afford to pay him the salary I'd offered would have told him the business was doing nicely, thank you. It wasn't a generous salary, by any means, but it was better than your typical computer fraudster could have expected straight out of prison.

"Don't need it. But one of the reasons I don't need it is that I've always been careful about money. And I like company—for a while at least."

"No boyfriend?"

"None that ever stayed. I get caught up in my work; they don't like it."

He was quiet for a minute or two. Then he said, "Are we making a mistake?"

"Maybe. If it goes wrong, it goes spectacularly wrong. David, you don't have to do this. I don't expect anything in exchange for the job."

He snuggled against me. "You were a perfect gentleman until last night. And that was hardly harassment."

"How much do you remember?"

"I thought I'd been woken up by someone groping me. I fought back, took him by surprise, managed to knock him down. I wanted revenge... And then I really woke up, and it was the same man I'd been fighting, only I knew who you were and where I was. I wasn't back in prison."

I supposed that the hug could have been felt as an attack by someone who had reason to be paranoid about such things. "Pretty much what happened. You must have been in the sort of dream state where you're aware of what's going on around you, but you weave it into the dream."

He turned away from me briefly to set his mug down next to mine before leaning against me again. "You were only doing this, though, weren't you? I remember it clearly, and I understand now what you were actually doing." He looked troubled. "At least, I think I remember it clearly. I have a continuous memory—I was aware of things right from when I hit you, but I suddenly realised that I was awake and that I hadn't been a second before."

"Do you do this often?" If this was going to be a nightly or even weekly event, he needed help. More help than I could give him.

"Nightmares, and a few times I've woken sitting up or even standing next to the bed. But not like this."

"Might be just the change in environment. But if it happens again, I want you to see a doctor." Actually, that was one of the things he should be doing if he was staying. "You ought to register at the practice anyway."

"Do you want me to have an AIDS test?" he asked abruptly.

Good thing I'd finished my tea; I'd have choked on it. "Do you need one?"

"I don't trust the prison doctors," he said. "They had an incentive to lie. I could sue if I was infected as a result of prison negligence."

He probably could, if it had been a result of assault. Sexual or otherwise. "Condoms are a good idea anyway. But have a test if you're worried about it."

"I'll make an appointment on Monday." He sat up straight and clambered off the bed. "Time for breakfast, I think."

By the time I'd got out of bed and found my dressing gown, he'd already laid the kitchen table for breakfast. Not trying to ingratiate himself with me, I thought, but behaving like a flatmate rather than a lodger. Taking a fair share of the work, now that he had some idea of where everything was.

"Just cereal and toast?" he asked.

"Porridge, I think. Go and get the post from downstairs while I make it."

He brought back my usual stack of mail and a large envelope for himself. Several smaller envelopes fell out when he slit it open. "Forwarded mail," he explained.

Most of it looked official or business. I recognised the style of one or two envelopes. "You still have your bank accounts?"

"Savings accounts and cheque account." He grinned, a little wryly. "Not the credit cards, though."

And a prison address wouldn't help. "Maybe we should go to the post office and get you a box," I suggested. "You can use this address, but you might want one under your own control." I put his porridge in front of him. "Here, get that down you."

He tackled the porridge without paying any attention to it, reading through his post instead. I'd have felt miffed but assumed that porridge, even properly cooked porridge, didn't come under the heading of a newly rediscovered culinary delight. I poked through my own post, sorting it into piles to deal with later. One or two queries about potential work looked interesting, and I set those on top of the pile.

"Brendan?"

"Mm?"

"Can we go shopping? I could do with getting some more clothes."

He hadn't arrived with much; that was true. "Do you need money?" I was willing to bankroll him a little, since one of the reasons he needed more clothes was to present a respectable appearance to clients.

"No. It's going to be a bit awkward having to use cheques for everything, but I do have a cheque book and money in the account. And a small grant when I left prison, just enough to pay for a few nights in a hostel."

Maybe I should have asked for rent upfront. But then, the chequebook had only just arrived, to judge by one of the envelopes. "What happened to your stuff from before?"

He waved a letter at me. "Friend put some of it in her attic. But she won't be able to get down here with it for a couple of weeks at least."

He had at least one friend willing to stand by him, then. "Girlfriend?"

"Just friend." He smiled in reminiscence. "She thinks I'm an idiot. She's right. But she helped as well as nagged." He looked at me. "All right if I use the phone, let her know what's going on?"

"Didn't you tell her?"

"Just that I had a possible job when I got out, so I wouldn't need to embarrass her by dumping myself on her." He collected his post together and stood up. "I've had my shower, so I'll go and get dressed. I'll do the dishes while you're in the shower."

He disappeared in the direction of his bedroom, leaving me to wonder about the friend who was not a girlfriend, but who would have given him a home if he'd needed it.

AS PROMISED, THE dishes were sitting neatly in the drying rack when I got out of the shower. I dressed quickly, and we were out of the house by half ten. It felt slightly odd to be walking to the shops with this man who was not my lover, but who would be. I was a little easier in my mind about that now that I knew he had somewhere else to go, but I wanted to check. "David, if you don't want to stay here, will your friend give you somewhere to stay?"

"For a few weeks. Why?"

"I'd be happier about the whole situation if I knew you could leave if you wanted to."

"I still wouldn't have a job."

"But you'd have somewhere to live."

He stopped walking and looked at me. "Brendan, you've been good to me. Better than I've a right to expect, after last night. I don't *want* to go."

He took my hand in his and squeezed it. "It felt good when you held me, and I wasn't thinking that I had to let you. I was just glad to have someone who *would* hold me and not ask a price for it."

Then he let go of my hand, and we went on our way. He seemed less nervous of crowds this morning and was enjoying wandering in and out of shops. We sorted out a post office box for him and got him not just registered at my doctor's surgery but an appointment for Monday afternoon. We ended up in a cafe for a late lunch, partly because David was clearly getting tired and in need of a sit-down.

"It's cheap and cheerful," I said, "but they use good quality ingredients and cook it nicely."

"Sounds good."

He wrapped himself around a toasted cheese sandwich and took a ridiculously childish delight in having a mug of hot chocolate with a couple of marshmallows in it. We talked about the area, me telling him about the local amenities.

"I'd like a walk in the park," he said, a little wistfully.

So after lunch, we walked in the park, kicking through the autumn leaves that were just starting to fall. Traditional old-fashioned romance, and I was enjoying it enormously. We stood and watched the ducks on the pond for a while, David regretting not having brought some bread.

"Tomorrow," I promised. "Or next weekend." He was shivering a little but didn't seem to want to leave, so I stood behind him and put my arms around his waist.

He leaned back against me, draping his arms over mine. "It's nice to live somewhere where we can do this."

"You get the odd moron. But most people wouldn't say anything, even if they don't like it." I rubbed my cheek against his hair. It was beautifully soft, which explained something about why I'd had to add conditioner to the shopping list this morning. "If we were snogging, they'd probably have something to say about it, but this won't get anything more than a few stares."

"I suppose we'd better get going," he said, sounding reluctant.

"We've still got the grocery shopping to do, even if you don't want to go back and pick up any of the clothes you were looking at."

"I'm getting tired. Let's get the groceries and go home."

ONE THING I hadn't put on the grocery list. I didn't expect to need it for a while, but it would be as well to make sure I actually had some in stock that were guaranteed not to be past their expiry date. I headed down the pharmacy aisle, David in tow. He raised an eyebrow at me when he realised where I'd stopped. "Feeling optimistic?"

"Being practical. I don't expect to need them this week, but it would be very annoying if we wanted them and didn't have any."

He grinned at me, and my heart turned over once again. "There are other things we can do."

"And we'll probably do them first," I reassured him. "But do you want to have to stop if we get carried away?"

"Can't imagine you getting carried away about anything." He started to browse, picking up a packet to inspect the details.

"I was thinking of getting carried away over a steak dinner tonight. Prime fillet, mushrooms, peas, and mashed potato? How does that sound?"

"Wonderful. You're far too good to me."

"I said I was careful with money, not that I won't spend it. I'm quite happy to spend it on things I'll actually enjoy." I picked up a different brand. "So if you want the most expensive, kinkiest brand, go ahead." I wasn't quite sure that glow-in-the-dark would actually add anything to the experience, but it might be amusing.

"Like me?"

"Like you. I enjoy watching you enjoying things."

We were getting some odd looks from a couple of women browsing the shampoo bottles. I stared them down. If they didn't like gays, that was their problem. I turned back to the condom stand, picked up a different packet, and said, "This one's suitable for anal sex," at a volume that wasn't loud, but wasn't exactly shy and retiring, either.

David smirked slightly. "Although I think I'd quite like to use these ones with knobs on."

"Whatever you like, my pet."

"Dirty old man," one of the women muttered, in a whisper intended to be overheard.

David looked as if he'd like to collapse laughing but restrained himself. He grabbed a tube of lube and dropped it in the trolley along with a couple of different types of condom. "Let's go and pick out the steak."

Once we were safely clear, I grumbled about people not keeping their prejudices at home.

"Brendan, they weren't objecting to gays. They think you're my sugar daddy." David looked as if he was still having trouble keeping a straight face.

I stopped walking, gobsmacked. I simply hadn't thought about the age difference—the impression it might make if I was the one obviously paying for everything. I ran back over the conversation and was mortified. If someone didn't know what the real situation was, that was exactly what they might have thought.

David tucked his hand around my arm. "I know you're not, Brendan. There's a difference between generosity and trying to buy people, and I know the difference."

"Thanks." I was glad of the reassurance. I didn't want to buy David, with money or with the job.

He looked serious now. "People will think it, though. You're old enough to be my father."

Forty-nine wasn't *that* old. But he was right; I was twice his age, quite literally old enough to be his father. "Does it bother you?"

"No. Sober and sedate looks very appealing to me now."

I decided that it was probably a compliment, on balance. I supposed there was another reason for him to prefer an older man. "And I have better control of my libido."

"That too," he said quietly. "It helps. A lot."

Because I was old enough to understand that erections were not the most important thing in the world. That they could be ignored, if necessary. "Let's go and find our steak."

"I do a rather nice blackberry crumble," David offered. "It's a good night for something like that."

"Better make it a small steak, then."

We finished our shopping and headed to the checkout. Of course, it would be the two old bats behind us in the queue. David flicked a glance at them and then asked me, "What work do you have planned for Monday?"

"There are a couple of promising queries for new projects. I'll spend the morning following them up. I want you to do some background research on the net for a client; she's worried about an investment and wants me to dig into it, but it's not quite my field."

"See if there's anything in Trading Standards reports, whether there's something odd about the website registrations, things like that?"

"Exactly." We might be winding up the old biddies, but it was a serious conversation. "You've got more experience at that type of work than I have."

"You look pretty comfortable with computers to me."

"For an old fogy, you mean? Young man, just because I learnt my programming skills on a mainframe—"

"Doesn't mean you need a Zimmer frame." He patted my bottom and added, "Boss."

Which was probably giving an even worse impression, but I was too busy enjoying having my bottom patted to care.

The checkout girl smiled at us as she flipped the condoms past the scanner. "Have fun, boys."

David turned pink. It was rather sweet, especially after the way he'd handled the old biddies. He hurried around to pick up the bags while I paid for the shopping. I took one bag from him, pointing out that I was not too decrepit to carry my own shopping, and we made our way home.

It was definitely a good day for a blackberry crumble. One of those fine autumn days—clear sky and still air so that it was a warm afternoon, but you could tell that it was going to turn chilly as soon as the sun went down. We'd been out most of the afternoon, and David decided to start on the crumble as soon as we'd unpacked the groceries and had a cup of tea. It was nice having someone pottering about the kitchen, and never mind the potential for sex.

"You like cooking?" I asked.

"Mm." He was concentrating on getting the texture of the crumble mix right, obviously knowing exactly what he wanted to achieve and how to achieve it. "It was one of the things I missed. Funny what you don't realise is important until it isn't there anymore."

"Gardening?" I guessed, thinking about what he'd wanted to watch on TV.

"That wasn't so bad once I was in the open prison."

"We can do a bit of gardening tomorrow," I suggested. "I need to get some of the autumn jobs done."

He looked up at me and smiled. "I'd like that."

Strange situation, this. Domestic bliss, as if we'd lived together for years. Yet he was fresh out of prison; I'd only met him a week before. No wonder the old biddies had jumped to conclusions. "Don't forget to phone your friend," I reminded him.

I wanted him to have that outside tie, somewhere else he knew he could go. Sensible as he was about the situation, he'd still felt he hadn't had a choice about the job.

"As soon as this is done."

I didn't hear what he said to her; as soon as he'd finished making the crumble, I told him to go and phone her while I tidied up for him. After that, I started preparing the main course. It was a convenient excuse to give him some privacy, but I didn't want to leave the meal too late anyway. He wandered back into the kitchen about twenty minutes later, saying, "Sorry about that, but she wanted to talk."

"If she's the good friend she sounds, she'll want to make sure you're all right. How do you like your steak?"

"Rare side of medium. Anything I can do to help?"

"Set the table."

He didn't have to ask where the steak knives were. It occurred to me that if he hadn't been the man he was, that might not have been a pleasant idea. Still, if I'd been worried about being murdered in my bed, I wouldn't have offered him a room. Or I'd have at least asked him to move elsewhere, instead of locking my door at night.

"David, did you do any more sleepwalking last night?"

He looked down at the knife he held. "Not that I'm aware of," he said with careful emphasis. He looked at the heavy knife I was using to slice the mushrooms. "Maybe you should lock the kitchen at night."

"It's not you I don't trust, it's your subconscious."

He set the steak knife down in its correct place. "I don't trust it either. Lock the door tonight, Brendan. I'll talk to the doctor about it on Monday."

It would be annoying, but I'd lock the kitchen at night until we were reasonably sure there would be no more episodes like last night. He'd only been out a week, so it might take him a while to adjust. Pity, I quite liked the idea of being brought tea in bed.

The steak was excellent, and David had learnt to slow down and enjoy his meal now. Tonight I could openly watch him enjoy it—could take pleasure in his sensual enjoyment. There was nothing flirtatious about his behaviour, just appreciation of good food. He picked up on my interest and said, "You meant it about having fun watching me enjoy myself, didn't you?"

"Yes. People always assume an accountant must be a dry stick who doesn't get a kick out of anything. I like the things my money can buy me; I like watching my friends get a kick out of them." I sighed, thinking about the sort of stupid little nitpicks that had caused me to invite previous lodgers to leave. "Too many people don't stop to *enjoy* life. Busy, busy, busy. No time to properly taste a meal, got to be doing something *useful* with the time, or it's been wasted."

"Protestant work ethic gone mad," David said. "I saw a lot of that. People eating at their desks, instead of going to the canteen or out to a cafe, not because they wanted to read a book or play a computer game for half an hour, but because they weren't *contributing* if they weren't constantly working."

"You had to be dragged away from your desk," I pointed out.

"That's different. I *enjoy* my work, and I've been deprived of it for the last year."

Good food, a walk in the park, and work that was fun. Yes, he might well have thrown himself into the work simply because he'd missed it.

"I often ate in front of the computer," he said. "But only because what I was doing was too interesting to stop, not because I had to prove what a devoted employee I was."

Ouch. I was getting a picture of David's former workplace that explained something about why he'd been so easily corrupted. "Try not to do too much of that here."

He smiled at me. "I didn't realise how much I *was* being pressured until I came here and was reminded what it's like to work somewhere where you're allowed to have a personal life. It's easy to get sucked in."

"Even if the private and work life overlap rather a lot," I said, thinking of having my bottom patted by someone who was calling me "Boss" at the time. "Do you think we scandalised them even more when they realised that I was not your sugar daddy but your lecherous old boss?"

The smile turned into a smirk. "I do hope so."

"You are a very naughty little boy. How's the crumble?"

He glanced at the oven. "Should be ready in five minutes."

"The last lodger thought pot noodles were appropriate fare for single men living in lodgings. You are a distinct improvement."

"Good." He stood up and started clearing the plates away. I let him get on with it; I didn't want him taking on all the work but wasn't going to make a point of it. Simpler just to go and fetch the dishes for the crumble.

He *was* a good cook—at least of blackberry crumble. It was hot and filling and very satisfying on a cold evening. Afterwards, I made tea while he did the washing up, and then we took the tea through to the sitting room. I'd lit the fire earlier, and the room was pleasantly warm.

"Gas fire?" David asked. "It's very realistic."

"Yes. There's a real coal fire in the other room, as an emergency backup, but this looks like the real thing and doesn't need any work to look after. It's handy for days when it's not been cold enough to put the central heating on." Although I'd probably put the heating on tonight or tomorrow. "I'd better check the forecast, see if we're going to need the central heating."

It was just before the hour; I should catch the forecast on the radio. I turned it on, but it turned out to be only the headlines, with no weather forecast. It would have to be television or wait until the next hourly news.

"Leave it on?" David asked as I stood up. "I'd like to listen to it."

"All right. I'll put the TV on for a minute to check the weather."

Cold but fine, apparently. Probably worth having the heating on. I turned the TV off again and went to set the system. When I got back, David was leaning back in the sofa, eyes closed. Awake, I thought, but concentrating on the radio.

I turned the main lights off, so the room was lit only by the fire and one small side lamp. That was the other nice thing about the fire; it looked exactly like a real coal fire unless you looked very closely, and you *felt* warmer looking at it.

"Brandy?" I asked quietly.

He thought about it for a few seconds. "Very small one, please."

I poured two glasses and went back to the sofa and nudged David's foot with mine. "Here."

He opened his eyes and took his brandy from me. I settled down next to him, watching the fire as I sipped at mine. After a few minutes, he edged over to lean against me, not saying anything; apparently still listening to the play on the radio. I was only half listening, more enjoying the play of voices against one another than paying attention to the plot. I put my arm around him, settling him against me more comfortably.

A quiet evening with a warm fire, a warm brandy, and a warm body to hold. There are worse ways to spend a Saturday night.

It took quite a long time to finish our drinks, and we finished more or less together, although I'd given him less than half of what I'd had. I took his glass and went into the kitchen to rinse the glasses out, leaving him still listening to the play. I was pleased he didn't try to do this bit of housework.

He fitted. He fitted into my life as if there'd been a David-shaped hole that I just hadn't noticed. Yes, he was half my age, but the experience of prison had made him older than his years. He was *trying* to fit in, not to ingratiate himself with me, but as a simple matter of learning to live with someone else. He understood my work and shared my enthusiasm for it even though he came at it from a different perspective. He'd seen immediately how to map his own field of expertise onto it. He'd been on the receiving end of my own sort of expertise but didn't seem to resent that and, in fact, was thrilled by the idea of being poacher turned gamekeeper, even if he hadn't consciously put it to himself in those terms yet. I might just have the partner I'd been looking for, however disreputable the way he came to me.

"You, Brendan"—I told myself—"are a lucky old sod, even if you will have to keep the doors locked at night for the next few weeks."

I went back to the sitting room—and David. This time, he cuddled up to me as soon as I sat down, his head resting on my shoulder. I was a little uneasy, reminded of the night before, but he seemed happy enough.

I'd thought he might fall asleep after all the exercise today, but he was still awake when the play finished. We listened to the news headlines, and then I got up and switched the radio off.

When I sat down again, he was sitting upright. Eyes shining in the firelight, lips slightly parted. An invitation if ever I saw one, but not one I was accepting without checking first. "David?"

He came willingly into my arms, kissing me lightly. Then he pulled away slightly, looking doubtful. "I want to, but…"

I put up a hand to stroke his cheek. "David, if you want to stop, I can always go and have a wank. Don't worry about it. We can stop right now, or we can stop at kissing, or we can stop at petting. Whatever you're comfortable with."

He smiled shyly. "Actually, a wank sounds like a nice idea." He put his hand up to my face, brushing my fringe to one side. "The brandy's had a better effect on me tonight. I feel relaxed."

Brandy, and the quietly soothing firelight, and the comfort of being held with no pressure to perform. "I really didn't expect you to be up to anything."

"Neither did I. Let's make the most of it, shall we?"

Satisfied he'd tell me if it got too much for him, I kissed him. Gently at first; then more pressure. I could feel him trembling slightly, but he was only nervous, not really afraid.

Then his mouth opened under mine, inviting me in. I carefully explored him with my tongue, wanting to lose myself in this but not daring to risk missing any sign he was uncomfortable. He tasted of fine brandy, the brandy he'd sipped appreciatively. I prayed that tonight it would do no more than relax him.

His hand was twisted in my jumper, holding me as if he was afraid he'd lose me. He was breathing faster now, even panting a little. I stroked his chest carefully, waiting to see how he reacted. He squirmed closer, almost climbing into my lap.

I eased my hand lower, ready to stop if I had to. He flinched a little, but when I stopped kissing him for a moment, he said, "No. Go on." So I fumbled with his fly, getting it undone in the end, and reached inside his trousers. He was only half-erect. Half was better than nothing; at least he was getting something out of this. I managed to get his cock out, careful not to let the zip snag on delicate skin, and wrapped my hand around it. No movement, no teasing, just holding it comfortably as I went back to kissing him.

He sighed a little and settled back into accepting my kisses, passive but willing, his hand still wrapped tightly in my jumper.

He still wasn't completely hard when he let go of my jumper and tackled my trousers, but I had no doubts about his eagerness to get his hand on my cock. I certainly didn't have any problems with getting an erection; perhaps not as often as I'd like, but the sweetness of tonight's unexpected pleasure had already brought my cock to attention.

Then he finally matched me in hardness, and I stroked him slowly and a little gently, at first. He was hesitant in his initial reply, and then gaining in confidence, gave good hard strokes the length of my cock. Eagerly kissing me back now, not just welcoming me.

He wanted me; he really wanted me. He was still scared, but he trusted me enough to let me do this, believing in my promise to him. I clutched him to me, squeezing his cock hard in my hand, and he responded with a squeeze of his own, breaking the kiss long enough to say "Want you, Brendan," in a hoarse tone. And with that, I came, revelling in the feel of his hand milking my cock.

I must have set him off, because the next thing I noticed, other than how good it felt, was how my hand was wet and sticky now.

Finally, I relaxed back against the sofa. I looked ruefully at the state of my trousers. "Laundry day tomorrow, I think."

He looked at his own mess. "Are any of those clothes shops open tomorrow?" he asked plaintively.

"I suppose we should have been more careful."

"If we'd stopped to be careful, I probably wouldn't have got started again."

"Are you all right?" I asked.

He nodded and smiled. "No nightmares tonight, I think."

"I'm surprised you're still awake." I stroked his hair with my clean hand. "Actually, I'm surprised you stayed awake long enough for us to get round to that. You've had a tiring day."

He stretched and stood up. "I was enjoying being with you. It was a nice evening, even before..." He gestured at his cock. "But I think I'd better go and get out of these clothes."

"You know where the laundry basket is. Want some hot milk?"

"Yes, thanks."

I stopped off just long enough to put two mugs of milk in the microwave and then went to change. David was in the kitchen when I got back, also in pyjamas and dressing gown. He came over to me and hugged me. "Even if it doesn't work out—thank you for tonight, Brendan. It means a lot to me."

I watched as he picked up his milk and left. It had meant a lot to me too.

I went downstairs to put the front door of the flat on the deadlock and pocket the key. Then I picked up my own milk and locked the kitchen door behind me. No sense in taking chances, even if David had gone to bed a lot happier than he'd been at the start of the week. It was a nuisance, but it was well worth it.

It might not work out. We might decide in the end that we'd made a mistake. But we'd have a damned good try at it first.

A Sparrow Flies Through

THE ONLY GOOD thing that could be said for the evening was that it wasn't as cold as it might have been. I was standing in a godforsaken London square, with the rain tipping down outside the cracked plastic of the bus shelter. Half the street lights in view weren't working, and the only spot of brightness was the light on the superloo occupying prime position directly across the road from us.

The other half of "us" had dashed into the dubious delights of the bus shelter thirty seconds after I had and joined me at the timetable. We'd done the careful dance of the Englishman trying not to get in someone else's way in a confined space. Some squinting had ascertained that we both had fifteen minutes or so to wait until the next bus on our respective routes. Not bad at this time of night, really. Now we were amusing ourselves reading the advertising posters plastered to the outside of the superloo.

Maintaining a polite silence wasn't helped by the poster slap in the middle of the loo's wall. I couldn't help laughing as I read it. In very, very large print it proclaimed, "They're coming!!!"

My new companion laughed as well and said, "I'm glad I'm not the only one with a filthy mind."

Implicit permission for conversation having been granted, I looked directly at him. "A poster like that on a public toilet—it's practically an invitation to go cottaging."

"The modern ones don't look much like a cottage. More like something out of Dr Who."

I looked him over. Older than I'd thought, late twenties. Smooth dark hair and pale skin, impossible to tell the actual colour in the orange glow of the street lights, but what I could see looked good. Smart clothes that looked as if he'd regret not having a raincoat with him tonight. And he had a sense of humour.

"Fancy seeing if modern technology beats the good old-fashioned way?" I asked.

"If nothing else, it's warm, well-lit, and dry," he said. "At least for the ten minutes it allows you before it opens the door and starts cleaning itself down." He grinned. "Of course, I'm not planning on using the full ten minutes."

I like long and leisurely myself, but I'm not averse to a quickie. "Got a twenty pence piece on you? Afraid I haven't."

He rummaged in a pocket and then triumphantly held up a coin. We sprinted for the superloo. Warm, well-lit, and dry. Well worth twenty pence on a night like this, even without a shag. In fact, it was well enough lit for a good look at what I'd got. Black hair and blue eyes—unusual combination.

Cheerful grin as well. "Like what you see?" he asked.

"Yes." I put a hand on his crotch. "Like what I feel, as well."

"And just where else would you like to feel it?"

This one appealed any which way. Lovely handful of hard cock, nice firm body. Gorgeous arse, I'd seen that much as I'd sprinted across the road behind him. Which did I want more—him fucking me, or me fucking him? Quick decision. "Up me. Got a condom?"

"As a matter of fact..." He rummaged in an inside pocket of his jacket, giving me a brief view of an expensive shirt stretched across a powerful chest. Fit without being a bodybuilding fanatic—just my type. He found the condom and offered it to me. "Thought I had one. Be prepared; that's my motto."

"Ex-Boy Scout?"

"Ex-Army, actually," he said. Well, that explained the physique.

I needed both hands to open the packet, so I had to let go of him. Only for a minute, I told myself. He got his trousers open while I got the condom open, and my, was his cock a pretty sight! Big, but not too big, nice satisfying thickness rather than all length. I wanted to get my hands on it again. Hell, I wanted to get my mouth on it. But not quite as much as I wanted to feel him filling my arse.

So I contented myself with stroking his cock as I rolled the condom down its sleek length. I'm good at that, even if I do say so myself. Lots of other people have said it as well. It's easier to persuade another bloke to wear a condom if you make sure he has a bloody good time out of it going on.

This bloke didn't actually say it, just hissed in pleasure, as I fingered his balls and then slid the last inch or two down with my hand wrapped tight around his cock. I'd have gone on my knees and used my tongue to help it down, but that takes longer, and I'm not one for giving public performances. I liked the thrill of knowing that the timer on the door was ticking, but only because I was certain I could beat it.

His hands were on me now, well-practised fingers opening my fly without fumbling. Trousers down far enough and then the usual undignified shuffling to get into position, trying not to trip over the fixtures and fittings. We got ourselves lined up, and I found myself looking at him in the mirror. He grinned at me and said, "Very kinky."

"Only if the mirror went down to the floor."

The grin got broader. "I must remember to suggest it at the next design meeting. You all right without lube?"

"Should be enough on the condom," I said. I'd noticed he liked a prelubed brand. "But suggest a hand cream dispenser at the design meeting."

He laughed, and then he stuck a couple of fingers under the tap before sticking one of them up me. "Just to be on the safe side." Finger out, cock in. Slowly, carefully, and I could see in the mirror what it was costing him. Almost too big for me, but not quite, filling me up. Then I had it all, and we paused for a second or two. He was pressed up against me now, and I could feel the heat of him against my back even through the light waterproof I was wearing. Then he wrapped his hand around my cock, squeezing and tugging at the same time. I was suspended between wanting to thrust forward into his hand and wanting to push back against his cock. He pulled out a little, pushed in again. Harder the next time, and faster, making me moan in pleasure.

A strange thing to be standing here in the clean bright light of the superloo, with the clean bright smell of the disinfectant, and this stranger's hand on my cock and his cock up my arse. Not like the old-style cottaging at all, no. No broken light bulbs or stale smell. But very good, with him hammering into me, tugging on me, and all the while the mirror showed me his manic grin.

I could finally see the point of mirrors, the pair of us feeding off each other's reactions. I gasped in pleasure, and so did he, and then he managed to nibble my ear while still looking at me in the mirror. Perfect timing, just when I'd enjoy it, rather than thinking it a distraction, and I slammed my arse back against him.

"Oh, no, you don't," he whispered in my ear. "We're coming together."

Ambitious, perhaps, but a nice idea. I let him set the pace, him rocking inside me and squeezing my cock. Me encouraging him with a few squeezes of my own.

Then he said, "Harder," and I obliged. I could feel the come rising in my cock. Then he buried his face against my shoulder, nuzzling at me. And we did it—we came together. Him clutching me tight, with an arm around my waist and a hand around my cock, as I spurted come against the sink.

The small bright room smelt a little more human now, even if only for the few minutes before the self-cleaning cycle started. And that was a reminder that the timer was still ticking.

I nudged the man still leaning on me. "Better get cleaned up."

"Before we get cleaned up whether we like it or not?" He disentangled himself from me with a look of regret. "You take first crack at the sink."

"Thanks." I made myself respectable and then waited as he did the same. Then we hit the door release and sprinted for the bus shelter. Just in time really because both buses turned up early.

One last request from him. "Lend us a few coins? That was part of my bus fare, and the driver probably won't give me change for a tenner."

I found a handful of coppers and passed it over, and that was the last I saw of him. Maybe if the buses had been late... But they hadn't and there'd been no time for conversation. Just one brief moment of warmth and light in a dark cold night, a memory to carry away.

I climbed onto my own bus and settled into a seat where I could watch the superloo automatic cleaning cycle finish erasing the evidence that we had ever existed.

AND IF I OFFERED

THEE A BARGAIN

THEY SAY YOU can't go back, and some places I don't want to. Not to Belfast, my home town though it is. And not just for the obvious reason, though I was glad enough to get away from that. The place has changed, mostly for the better, but in some ways for the worse, and I can't stick seeing the worse.

I escaped into the frontiers of the mind long before I escaped in body, the local library being well-stocked in science fiction. Imaginary worlds were my refuge, whole universes for my delight. But escape in body I did, eventually, away to England and university and a job. Still, Belfast draws you back, if only for a few days' visit. And so I found myself one fine day wandering the countryside, the road winding in and out and over the drumlins of County Down, and Strangford Lough appearing and disappearing with the twists and turns of the road.

I turned inland after a while, which was a mistake, for I didn't have a map and didn't know the roads as well as I'd thought. You know how it is: the roads look different when you're the driver and not the passenger. Still, it took me past some things I had not seen before, at least not that I could recall, and eventually I found a pleasant spot to stop and have a cup of tea from the thermos in the car. A green hillside, with not a soul around, where I could sit and admire the view. There was a narrow path around the hill, with a public right-of-way sign, so I need not fear trespassing. I climbed a little up from the path and settled myself on the grass. I felt almost guilty at disturbing the quiet when I pulled out my mobile phone and set it to playing my current audiobook, but I was close to the end and wanted to hear it.

I must have dozed off in the warm sunshine, for I awoke with a start to find an alien standing before me. Black hair, white skin, and great gold eyes with a not quite human slant to them. And pointed ears. Why is it always pointed ears? I suppose because even the pro-grade prosthetics are relatively cheap and easy enough to come by, with the demand from the Trekkers, and they can be readily adapted for other fandoms, other mythologies. I'm sure he'd have frightened the mundanes, but I've seen odder things often enough. If I'd known there was a science fiction con on locally, I'd have made an effort to go to it.

Especially if I'd known there were fans as pretty as this one to be found there. Pretty he certainly was, even with the daft outfit. I felt my cock stir.

That, and curiosity, and politeness, suggested I find out who he was. "Where'd you spring from? It's a bit out of the way for a con, unless there's a conference hotel just over the hill." Although he wasn't wearing a membership badge. Another possibility struck me. "Or are you filming something?"

"None of those," he said, and his voice was as beautiful as his body. "I'm not from your world, Jack."

"Dark they were, and golden-eyed..."

"I don't believe in Martians," I said. "Or even Vulcans. It's a nice costume; they can do wonderful things with contact lenses these days, can't they?"

Wonderful things, and even the sclerals are almost comfortable these days, and you could have got the gold iris and the cat's-eye slit with a simple prescription-style lens. Except that I couldn't see the tape that had to be there to hold the eyes in the wrong shape.

"I don't bleed green, thank you," he said.

And how the hell had he known my name? I didn't have a stalker amongst the local fen—not that I knew of, anyway. Only I really didn't want to believe I'd been chosen for a 'first contact' situation by some species that had watched enough of our TV to catch the references.

"You'd have known me once, Jack," he said, "but your people have different tales of glamour to tell now, don't they?" He cocked his head on one side. "Your ancestors would not have been fool enough to sleep where you sleep now. Although I suppose the gateway warning isn't so clear nowadays."

"Gateway?"

"Door, perhaps." He gestured...and the hillside a few metres away from me opened up, the turf swinging up and out in two great leaves as if they were indeed the leaves of a door. I'm not ashamed to say that I yelped and scrambled to my feet, but there was a curiosity as well as fear pulling at me. Had I managed to fall asleep on a spaceship that had grown a lawn to disguise itself? I walked the few metres to the doorway and peered in—from what I hoped was a safe distance.

The turf was soil on the underside, and it had hidden a dark passage cut through the mound of the hill.

And then I knew who and what he was and was afraid. The Good People are called that for a reason, and I'm not so out of touch with my cultural heritage as to not know what it is. It's never a good idea to express your true opinion of those with power. No, stay away from the Fair Folk if you value your sanity and your life. Fair of face, indeed, but capable of cruelty and capriciousness. Even the ones with no malice in them have a way of forgetting that mortals are, well, mortal. They'll take you away for a year and a day, or even a year times seven, and have no thought for your own life.

Legends. Myths. Superstition.

Not real. We all know that, don't we?

Well, an old legend, an old warning, had sprung to new life, and the door was ajar in front of me. I stood in the warm sunshine and shivered as if the gentle breeze that blew from the opening had come straight from Antarctica.

Then there was a hand on my shoulder, and a voice like silver bells saying, "It will not suck you in, Jack. It must be your choice, to take that road." And he waved his hand again, and the doors closed themselves.

"It's probably not a good idea to leave it open, not in the day," he said. There was laughter in his voice as he added, "After all, it might frighten the mundanes."

"What do you want?" I could hear the fear in my own voice.

"You, Jack." He pulled me around to face him, and for the first time, I realised he was shorter than me. He'd given the impression when I'd been looking up at him, from my seat on the grass, that he was a tall man. He still did, and it was only the knowledge that I was actually looking down at him slightly that counteracted that. Glamour—it was the glamour—I found myself analysing.

"Me?"

He brushed the fingertips of one hand across my face. "You. You see me, and you believe, and you are not afraid."

Couldn't he bloody hear my heart hammering?

He smiled. "Not so afraid, at least, that you will not even listen to me." Then he leaned forward and kissed me.

Well.

He might be one of the sidhe, but he *felt* human enough against my mouth, and in my arms, and against my cock. And pressing me against the good green grass, where we had dropped, or fallen, in a tangle. And then he pulled away, and I could no longer feel him touching me.

I opened my eyes, wondering whether I was dreaming, whether it was only now that I was waking, and found that I was not. He was still there and still solid, only now he was crouching over me, watching me with a rather wistful expression on his face. "I think I may have made a mistake," he said.

"Mm?"

"I only came out because I wanted a little time in this world, and there was the chance to do so. I did not expect to find *you*."

"Why didn't you let me sleep on?" I asked. I was still afraid, but only of accidental damage now; I did not feel any malicious intent from him.

"Because your story came to an end, and I wanted to hear more." He glanced to one side. "I dare not touch it."

I followed his gaze. He was looking at the phone, which lay silent now. So that was what had attracted him. The old tales told of the sidhe being fascinated by bards, minstrels, the storytellers and singers. "It's only someone reading a written book aloud; it's not a true bard tale."

"But such a beautiful voice, and he knows how to use it." He looked at me again. "And we like your tales of wonder as much as we do our own."

I couldn't help laughing at that.

"What's so funny?" he asked, looking bewildered.

"Well, I thought you were a science fiction fan when I first saw you. Don't tell me you actually are one!"

He smiled, dazzling me. "Yes, I see." He stroked one hand down my T-shirt—the one from a con the year before. His touch made me tingle. "Well, if I could walk in your world for a whole weekend, I would spend it at one of these."

"You'd probably get away with it, too." I stroked him in turn, still reassuring myself that he was real and not some phantasm to turn to mist under my touch. "You could pass for a human in costume, if you were careful."

"One reason, although not the only one." Then he leaned down and kissed me again, making me dizzy. I barely heard what he said next. "I do like your science fiction, your fantasy. Your tales have changed, and the ways you can tell them, but they are still exciting."

"What's exciting me at the moment is you. Come here."

I grabbed him and pulled him down on me, wanting the contact. He came willingly into my arms, lying full length upon me. He was as aroused as I was, his cock hard against mine, his face flushed a little now. His body felt a little odd under my exploring hands, but well within the range for humans. Harder muscled than I'd somehow expected in such a slim body.

I looked up at him, still not quite sure I wasn't dreaming. Golden cat eyes looked back down at me, but no cat he—something far more alien. And very, very real. I thrust up against him without my even thinking about it first, my body taking over. He gasped, his eyes half closing, and then shoved against me before pulling back, one hand going to my trousers.

Common sense returned. "What if someone comes past?"

"Sod them." He grinned wickedly. "Although I'd rather sod you."

"*You* can vanish back inside your hill. I'll have to stay here and face the law. We're not supposed to frighten the horses, you know."

"I'll make them think they've been seeing things." He brushed his lips over mine, making it difficult to think. I stopped worrying about passers-by—after all, I'd deliberately picked a spot that was out of the way, that did not have a direct view of the road. And maybe he *could* glamour anyone who came by; he'd certainly managed to glamour me. No fear now, just desire for the attractive man in my arms.

"Anyway," he went on, "you can hide with me. Just inside the door holds no danger."

"We have these things called cars. With things called licence plates." It was possible that he didn't actually know, although his use of fannish terminology suggested recent contact with the modern world. "Mine's parked over there, which makes it easy for anyone who takes offence to trace who I am."

"A car, I'll admit, would be a more difficult thing to hide," he said. "But why would anyone want to trace it, if there's no call to know who the owner is?"

I believed him. So I made no further protest as he explored the fastening of my jeans, unzipping them and slipping his hand inside to grip my cock. Oh god, but the touch of his hand on me felt good, and I wondered whether it was just lust, or if there was true magic in it. I fumbled with his clothes in turn, only then noticing what I should have noticed—that they were ordinary clothes like mine. I had taken him for a stray con member because that's what he looked like, dressed in jeans and T-shirt, or something much like them. "*Zips?*" I asked incredulously.

"We like modern technology. At least that of it we can use. Plastic's wonderful—why didn't you people think of it earlier?" He grinned again. "I don't suppose you have any interesting sex toys with you? I'd like the chance to try one."

"I think *you* count as the most interesting sex toy I've ever had. And no, I've none with me."

I'd managed to get him out of his jeans by now and had no doubt at all that he was interested in me. His cock was hard and beautiful. There was something...not quite human...about the shape, but the difference was no more than the shock you get if you're used to uncircumcised men and you get one who is—the double take at it being not quite what you're used to—but keen enough on it for all of that. Like the rest of him, pointed ears and golden eyes and all—not homo sapiens, but human enough. I pushed at him, so that we ended up with him being the one lying on his back and me leaning over him. Then I leaned down and took him in my mouth, wanting to taste him, and yes, wanting to know whether he tasted different.

And he did taste different, although I could not have told you how. Different and wonderful, his cock filling my mouth as he grabbed the back of my neck and pulled me right down. I almost choked, and then he relented, his hand stroking me softly rather than forcing me. "I'm sorry," he said, "I should not have done that."

Reassured, I explored him with my mouth, savouring the slight differences. One thing was the same—the sound of a man gasping in pleasure as I licked and sucked at him. I'm good at it—I've been told so, often enough—but it was still something to let go and look back at his face and see his delight in what I'd been doing. The sidhe are said to have exacting standards, and no doubt that applied to lovemaking as much as to music making. "Good enough for you?"

"More than good enough, my Jack," and his voice caressed me even as his hands did. "Are you as good at other things?"

He tugged at my T-shirt—a less than subtle hint. I clambered off him, regretting the inelegance that haste and lust made of my movements, and pulled my T-shirt off. He'd sat up and done the same and was now wriggling out of his jeans. Even now I wondered whether that was wise, whether we would not be safer doing something that could be construed as cuddling, but I followed his lead.

And then we were naked before one another, and I marvelled at how beautiful he was. I knew it might be glamour and that I might not be seeing his true appearance, but I wanted him so badly that I didn't care. He was beautiful to me not just in looks, but in what he was—my own alien come to me, not from the stars but from out of legend.

I hoped I was the same to him, and then I saw the way he was looking at me and knew that I was. I was the alien, the wonder, to him. The touch of fantasy in his life.

"Jack, may I be on top?" he said, making of it a formal request.

A practical matter struck what was left of my mind. "Does your magic extend to not needing condoms and the like?" I had what was needful in my luggage in the car but no wish to get dressed again so that I could go to the roadside.

"Condoms we do not need." He rummaged in his pockets. "This we could do without, but why should we deprive ourselves of the pleasure of putting it on?" He handed me a small jar. "Skin cream, in case the sun was too hot, but it will do."

I took it from him, tried the lid. Plastic lid on a small glass pot, not unlike the cosmetics pots my sister used. I dipped a finger into the cream inside, testing it. It felt pleasant enough, and if he was willing to use it so was I. I scooped some out and applied it to him, enjoying the feel of it as I smoothed it on. Satisfied with my work, I handed the pot back to him and lay back on the grass.

He anointed me in turn, careful, considerate. Driving my desire ever higher. And then he was done, dropping the little pot to one side and moving into my arms, plunging into me as I embraced him. Fast and deep and almost painful, and then we had the knack of it, how to move so that the slope of the hill helped us rather than hindering. He *was* shorter than me; I wanted to kiss him but couldn't quite reach his mouth, and then he wriggled somehow so that it worked. Only for a moment before the strain became too much for him, and he pulled away again, but enough. Then I contented myself with running my hands over him, marvelling at the softness of his skin, the feel of the fine strands of his hair, even as he nuzzled at my neck.

"Too damned fast," he muttered. "Wanted to show you how good I can be, but I want you; can't wait."

"Make it feel like magic?"

He glanced up at me, his face almost savage now. "Want to make you not be satisfied with anyone else. Ever."

That sort of possessiveness I could deal with, so long as he didn't propose to make me want and then not satisfy me. I clutched at his shoulders. "Fuck me," I ordered, shocked to hear my own voice.

He did, driving hard into me, making me dig my nails into his skin, although I only realised that later. Hard and fast and then neither of us could hold back any longer as he said, "*Now*, Jack," in a voice that was no longer silver bells, but deep and bronze with desire. We came together, swearing, panting, clinging to each other.

There must have been magic in it, for it took rather a long time before I noticed that elves are actually quite heavy.

Not only that—I hadn't noticed the approach of an audience. A man was walking along the path around the hill. I stiffened again and not in a good way. "Shit!"

He put his hand over my mouth and twisted around to look where I was looking. "Be quiet," he commanded in a whisper.

It was too late to run; we would be seen even if we went into the hill. So I stayed where I was, wondering what my parents would think of the headlines in the paper. Only, the man kept on walking, with no sign of alarm. He was looking around him, enjoying the view, and his gaze swept right over us, yet he never saw us, never halted to shout at us.

I slowly relaxed and watched in fascination as he walked by only a metre or so from where we lay. There was an enormous grin all over my lover's face, and I didn't think it was just from what we'd been doing as the man had come around the hill. "Believe me now, don't you?" he whispered, very quietly.

The man did look around, then, and glanced in our direction, looking a little puzzled. But he still did not see us where we lay tangled in a sweaty, naked heap, and he merely shook his head and walked on towards the gate. Only when he had passed through onto the road, and his footsteps had died away, was the hand removed from my mouth.

"Easier to glamour only one sense at a time," he explained, although I'd understood that once I'd seen the man's reaction to his whisper. "Though it was a bit careless of me not to do all when we were so close to the path."

"Would he have even heard us, if we'd been a bit further up the hill?"

"Only the rustling of a mouse moving through the grass."

I looked up at him and marvelled. "Now that is magic."

"Being able to hide from mortals?"

"Being able to make love out in the open, under the sky, and not worry about being arrested."

He frowned then. "Is it still so bad here?"

"Believe it. Even if we were man and woman, we could have been in trouble. But..."

"Barbarians," he hissed. "It was ill-mannered of us not to go away from the path, but that was all."

Well, it *was* bad manners, as well as foolish, to have made love right where anyone walking the path could not have helped but see us. "We'd better dress or move. It's not fair on other people to stay here like this; they couldn't avoid seeing us if you forget and let the glamour slip, and it upsets people to come across naked people unexpectedly, even if they don't mind the idea."

He sighed and rolled off me. "True." He reached for his clothes. "Can we at least hold one another for a little while?"

"That we can probably get away with."

And that was what we did. We gathered ourselves up, and he took me to a large stone, warmed by the afternoon sun. I leaned back against it, and he snuggled up to me, resting his head on my shoulder. He wanted to see more of the phone, fascinated by it. I showed him an e-book. "It can hold dozens of books. More with memory cards."

"A whole library in the palm of your hand," he said, wonder in his voice. He reached his hand out to almost touch it, hesitated, and then said, "This is different." And then he touched it very lightly, snatching his hand away instantly as if he had expected to be burnt. Then back again. "I can hold it." Joy, pure joy in his voice. "It has no iron in it. Or not enough to harm. And yet it is electrical."

"Your people really can't stand iron?"

"It makes the world change shape, and we cannot find our way."

"Plastic case, semiconductors, and electrically shielded." Idle speculation from a con panel returned to me. "If you have an electromagnetic sense, this wouldn't bother you. Not much, anyway."

"I wish I could take it with me." He sat up, pulling away from me a little, turning to face me. "Will you come with me, Jack, for a little while?" he asked wistfully. "I cannot stay here—not for long."

"Why not?" For that matter—"Why are you never seen any more?"

"There is too much iron in your world now."

I didn't know whether he meant that literally or metaphorically or both and was afraid to ask. If I asked, he might tell me, and I wasn't sure I wanted to know. Perhaps they just couldn't stand our electricity grids.

Something finally occurred to me. "I don't even know your name."

"Fergal," he said simply.

I blinked at that. It seemed a somewhat plain name for something so exotic.

"Or at least that's how you would say it now."

"Just how old *are* you?"

He smiled slightly. "Not old at all, for my kind. Not even that old by your standards. Will you come with me, Jack? There are wonders I could show you, wonders I want to share with you as you have shared yours with me."

"And what's the price? I spend a night with you, and I come out and find that seven years have gone by?" No, I did not think him malicious, but I did think him perhaps not aware of how short my life was compared to his.

He shook his head. "We made a new bargain. I'll take you for seven years willingly enough, but it will be seven years in my world and only a night in yours."

"Fergal..."

"We learnt, Jack..." And his voice was bitter. "We learnt almost too late, what it was we had done to those we had loved. And we made a new bargain so that we might not harm you again. That price is no longer one you have to risk paying. You will be safe enough, if you obey the rules."

"Rules?"

"The gatekeeper will tell you. Will you come, at least as far as the gatekeeper, that he might do so?"

I trusted him, because he understood what it was I was afraid of. "All right." I looked at the phone I still held. "Shall I bring this?"

"You might have to leave it at the gate. But we should try. It would be a marvellous thing if we could have even one such. New stories..." And his eyes brightened.

"The laptop. I'll bring the laptop. The power won't last long, but if it'll work at all and it doesn't harm you, you can see a DVD." I got to my feet and went to the car, Fergal following me, but staying on the other side of the hedge away from the large lump of cold iron. And then we walked back to the hill, and the door and the tunnel leading somewhere that doesn't exist in the world. I held the laptop case in one hand, and his hand in the other, and as the door closed gently behind us, we walked down that tunnel into the light that shone from the far end.

There was another door—this one standing open—and another elf sitting there behind a small desk. Somehow, he felt older than Fergal, although he looked young in the face. He looked disapprovingly at Fergal.

"It's his own choice," Fergal said. "He wants to see and he has the strength of mind."

"And you're both young and in love and thinking with your balls," the older man snapped. "Have you two thought this through?"

In love? Yes, I was, although I had not thought of it until now. I had looked at him and known I wanted him. Had it been that way for him too? "Fergal said...that I would go back to my own world with nothing changed." Although, had he? "Will I have only aged a night?"

The gatekeeper nodded. "Time does not run the same in our worlds. Once, it was not predictable. It could be a day in each place, or a mortal lifetime in one while only a night in the other. But when we understood what we were doing to you, we made a bargain. And now time will not go faster in your world while you are here, and your body's age will be tied to your own time." He looked at us and sighed. "A pity that we did not think to ask if we could change one or two other things while we were at it. Love at first sight may be very romantic, but as a geas across the worlds, it has its drawbacks."

"It can't be helped now," Fergal broke in. "I heard, and I saw, and I was lost."

It sounded like a formula. The gatekeeper tutted at him and then looked at me again. "Do you understand what you are getting into?"

"Can I leave before the seven years are up?"

"The door will stay open for a night of your time, and you may come and go as you please. With or without this young idiot. After that... One night of your time, seven years of ours. Those are the terms. Do you accept them?"

How could I not? I'd always regret it if I turned on my heel and left. "Yes."

"What do you bring with you?"

It felt just like customs and security at an airport. I supposed that in a way it was. I put the laptop case on the table, and then my phone, and the contents of my pockets, and switched on the things that could be switched on. Fergal was almost babbling in his eagerness to convince the gatekeeper that they needed these things. The gatekeeper prodded at the laptop. "It's borderline. How much power can it put out?"

He clearly understood what he was talking about; perhaps they'd had trouble with electrical equipment before.

"I'll play a DVD," I offered. "That's the heaviest power drain." It started playing from where I'd left it. The Pan-Am shuttle to the moon—the first view of the monolith.

The gatekeeper was almost in tears. He looked at me. "Thank you for bringing us this. We have been told the story, and by fine storytellers, but I never expected to see it with my own eyes."

We passed inside, with everything I had brought.

I WAS MADE welcome, very much so, even before I showed them my toys. It seemed that we walked for miles—and yet I was not hungry nor thirsty nor tired—meeting the people of the land I was in. Distances didn't seem to work in the normal fashion, so it might have only been a few hundred metres instead. And then we sat down to a great feast that was prepared, and I set another audiobook going to entertain the diners, although I wondered whether it was wise to drain the battery like that. Only afterwards, as I checked to see what battery life was left, did I realise something. "Fergal, we've been here hours, and the time on this is the same as when we came in!"

He peered at it. "Maybe it's keeping the time of your world."

"But it's working at normal speed!"

He shrugged. "So are you. And you'll only be a day older when you go back."

I could see his point. I didn't like it, but I could see it. I could think, move, at what seemed to me to be a normal speed, and yet they had reassured me that I would only age at the same rate as the outside world. Maybe the phone could do the same.

I really only believed it a week later, when the machine was still showing an almost full battery and was of the opinion that four seconds had gone by. It had spent that week constantly on, with at least one of the sidhe scribbling away, making records of the stories it held. I had no idea where the laptop was—it had been carried away by a group of gleeful science fiction fans intent on working through my DVD collection. I assumed that it was in the same oddly functional state as the phone, as it had not yet been returned to me.

"I think you can stop worrying about the battery life," Fergal said. "Do you have any interesting porn on there?"

Well, of course I did, and very inspirational it was too.

And so I spent short days and long nights, and the reverse, though not in any orderly, seasonly fashion of slow change from one to the other. I told them stories, I sang them filks, and I did that which all of us do for our friends from other countries who've not seen the latest series—the plot summary.

And I made love, many a time. We wandered through his country and made love wherever we pleased, for there was no scandal in it there. Not for two men, or at least two men of his race; there was sometimes muttering at his having taken a human lover. Not racism, so far as I could tell, but what seemed to be a fear for us both. I asked, once, of the gatekeeper.

"It's not as it was, child," he said. "Our worlds are drawing apart; it becomes harder and harder to cross between them. And harder yet for someone from one to live in the other."

"I manage." The place was strange, not paying much attention to the laws of physics that I was familiar with, but beautiful for all of that. I missed my friends back home, yes, but not strongly, as if my emotions were tied to the passage of time outside, rather than the months it had subjectively been. And I had my love to keep me company, and new friends here.

"For a time. But you're used to living in strange worlds; you do better than most of your kin could." He seemed saddened. "Others have gone mad. When the door closes, and there is no contact; when they realise that they are truly alone with us, and that this place is not home..." He shook his head. "He should not have brought you here, glad though we are to have you." Then he smiled. "Tell me of space exploration. I should have liked to have gone on a rocket ship, to have the moon in a fixed orbit, where one may set out and know that it will be there when one arrives."

So I told the gatekeeper of sitting watching old film—one small step for a man—and watched him dream of taking one large step for elfkind, into a world that no longer allowed of his existence.

THERE WERE NO mirrors in that place; I could not see the passage of time in my face. No clocks, no reliable astronomy, no easy means for me to tell the time. One only had one's innate sense that time was passing, and even I could feel that, although they were more sensitive to it than I was. I was not surprised when Fergal came to me and told me that it was our last night together, according to the bargain we had made. One night for seven years.

"No. I don't want to leave you." Bitter cold clamped around me as I looked at him, pointed ears and golden cat eyes that were not a costume. "And you can't come with me, can you?" Even if he could survive a world of cold iron, could he survive its people and their interest in him?

"You go back now or not at all. And you cannot live for long in Faerie, my love, any more than I can live in your world. A brief visit, that is all." He touched his fingers to my forehead, and I fell in a swoon.

"AND I AWOKE and found me here on the cold hill's side."

I must confess, that was my first thought when I did indeed awake and find me on the cold hill's side, although nowadays one thinks of our own scourge, not the tuberculosis of Keats. I loved him, I trusted him, but I could not help but remember the tales of those who'd sickened and wasted away when the geas was broken, and they'd lost their immortal lover. So I was away first thing to a doctor for tests, which all came back clear. Well, not first thing—the very first thing I did was find two pieces of the real and mortal world—a newspaper to check the date and a mirror to check my face. I had not changed, nor had the world. Only one night, as he had promised.

It took me a little longer than that to realise the true price. The price for both of us. There was nothing obvious, not at first, only the longing to see him again—him and his world—and to begin with I could deal with that. I'm used to living half my life in worlds that don't exist, not in this dimension.

One night of my life in exchange for seven years with him. All the price he was required to ask and all the gift he was allowed to give. He did not tell me what the true curse was, and I did not think to ask the right question.

The door has not opened to me again. It never will.

STORM DUFFY

ANY PORT IN A STORM

I HADN'T PLANNED on spending Friday night getting fucked senseless by two hot guys. I hadn't planned on getting stuck in town after work, either, not when the snow was just starting to come down thick and fast.

And I really hadn't planned on getting soaked by someone's coffee while I was walking through Piccadilly Gardens towards the tram stop. Not his fault, though. No, the one I cursed was the dick who barged past us so that we stumbled into each other.

"Shit, I'm sorry!"

I looked up from the wet stain on my coat and recognised the man as someone I often saw in the local sandwich shop at lunchtime. "Not *your* fault. That dickhead..."

And then the PA crackled into life, announcing that the Bury tram was delayed due to frozen points.

"Oh, fuck. That's all I need."

My fellow soakee asked, "Your tram?"

"And I really don't want to stand around soaking wet in this weather." There went my plans for getting home early. "I suppose I'd better go and find a public toilet with a working hand drier."

He was silent for a second or two and then said, "Look, my flat's only at the bottom of Market Street. Come and get yourself dried off. I owe you at least a hot drink. Maybe dinner."

If he'd been a complete stranger, or it had been a warm night, or my own place had been closer, I'd have turned him down. But all I could think of was a warm flat and a hot drink just a five-minute walk away. "Thanks."

He set off at a rapid pace, saying, "I know you from somewhere."

"We have the same taste in sandwiches."

He broke into a grin. "And men."

Sitting in a cafe, watching a nice arse go past, looking up to see someone at the next table doing the same thing. "By the way, I'm Phil."

"I'm Steve." He dodged around a knot of shoppers. "You'd think people would want to get home with this weather."

"That bastard who knocked us over certainly wanted to."

"Let's hope he's waiting for the Bury tram."

That thought kept me warm until we reached the entrance to his apartment block. It was only one of the most expensive towers in Manchester, a soaring glass shard that looked down the length of Deansgate. "I'm impressed."

"My boyfriend's income, not mine."

The hope I hadn't even noticed until then fizzled away. Still, the offer of a hot drink and maybe dinner was welcome without any extras. "As long as it's warm and dry, I don't care who's paying for it."

But when we got through his front door, I cared. The boyfriend was home, and he was stunning. Tall, lean, blond, and with a beautiful mouth. Wearing clothes that had to be made to his measure—they fitted his measure so well.

He said, "Thought I'd get home early; it's a nasty night." Then he saw me and said, "And I see you've brought dinner with you."

The way he looked at me made it clear exactly what he meant.

I glanced at Steve, who looked embarrassed. "Sorry, Phil. Julian, I only brought him home because I spilt my coffee all over him. And I wasn't leaving him out there." He waved at the floor to ceiling window, with its magnificent view of the city—and the snowstorm.

Julian tensed up. "Ah. Sorry about that. I assumed..."

It was obvious what he'd assumed. "Do you two make a habit of getting in a takeaway on Friday night?"

That tall, lean body relaxed again. "Well, yes. Variety is the spice of life, and all that." He looked us up and down appraisingly. "But you're here to get dried off. Go and get those wet clothes off." He smiled reassuringly at me. "And then put some dry clothes on." He looked at the snow. "You're welcome to stay for dinner, regardless. No strings. Unless you already had plans?"

I decided without even thinking about it. "I didn't have plans." I looked Julian over, quite openly checking out his crotch. "But I think I do now." I started unbuttoning my coat.

Steve put his hand on the small of my back. "You sure? I really did only invite you back to get dried off."

"I can think of worse ways to get warmed up."

He slid his hand down to cup the curve of my arse. "Good. But let's get these wet clothes off."

I pulled off my coat. "Need to do something about this."

Julian said—"I'll sponge it"—and took it from me. Elegant hands, well cared for. I thought about those hands on my body and felt my cock push against my trousers. My *wet* trousers. Julian glanced down, and a tiny smirk touched the corners of his mouth.

Steve said, "Bathroom's this way."

I followed him, taking the opportunity to check out his arse. Not the first time I'd admired those tight buttocks, but tonight I wouldn't have to imagine them naked.

Normally I'd start unbuttoning from the top, making it a bit of a striptease. Not tonight. The wet trousers came off first, and quickly. Not that Steve seemed to mind, because he paused in his own unbuttoning to take a good look. "I didn't ask you home with ulterior motives—but I'm not too unhappy now about that guy shoving me."

"Neither am I."

My sweater and shirt I took more time over. Steve kept watching, assessing what he saw. Finally, he said, "You know, if I'd had any idea that you might be up for it..."

"You might have done more than nod in passing in the sandwich shop queue?" I looked him over. Compact body, shorter than his boyfriend, but more solidly built. Big cock, though thick, without being out of the ordinary in length. I wanted that cock—in my mouth or in my arse. But I'd liked the scenery even when it was fully clothed. The clothes hadn't hidden a shock of dark hair over a square-cut face with an engaging smile. "If you'd asked, I'd have probably said yes. Maybe even if you'd mentioned Julian."

He grinned. "That was why I didn't ask. Not with someone I might have to see at lunch the next day." He moved closer, close enough to run his hands down my chest. Cool hands, still chilled from outside. Like cold fire running over my skin, making the nerves tingle.

I pulled him in close for a kiss. I could taste just a trace of coffee. He kissed me back hard, tongue thrusting into my mouth, and pushed me back against the wall. The tiles against my back were cold, but I didn't care. Hard cock against mine, his hands twined in my hair. I moaned around his tongue, wanting more than I already had.

He pinned me against the wall for a moment more and then pulled back, giving me room to ease away from the chill of the tiles. "Sorry. You were cold enough already."

"It's okay."

He slid one hand down my back and further down to cup my arse again. Skin against skin now, nothing between us. I leaned in against him, shifting just enough to make it an invitation, and he eased his hand round to press a finger against my hole.

God, I wanted more of that, but said, "Is this fair on Julian?"

Steve smiled. "He was serious about us getting out of our wet clothes. And I might as well get you ready while we're in here." He let go and stepped back. "Bend over."

I leaned on the vanity unit, watching in the mirror as he squeezed some cream into his hand. Then he slid a finger into me. Just one finger at first. Then another, pressing deeper, deep enough to make me gasp with pleasure. "Enough, if you want me to last!"

"If you're that desperate, you're probably out of practice." But he eased off, giving me a little respite so that I didn't feel as if I needed to thrust against something, anything, even the edge of the vanity unit.

He was right about the being out of practice, so I did my best to hold still while he worked me to make sure I was ready. Then he pulled out. "All right?"

"Mmm." That should be enough to make it easy to take even his thick cock. "Now what?"

"Now we see if Julian has laid the table." He quickly rinsed his hands. "Ready?"

I thought he was being metaphorical. He wasn't.

The lights in the main room were turned off, the only light in the room coming from the city lights below. Julian was standing by a dining table set up near the picture window, placed so that the diners could look out over the magnificent view. And the table was laid with a white damask tablecloth. No cutlery, I was very pleased to see. Just the heavy white cloth, shimmering in the flickering light reflected by the snow dancing outside the window.

Julian's pale skin gleamed in that same eerie light, making him look a little unreal in that first second or two. And then the scene steadied, and I was looking at just a naked man standing by a table. Tall and lean and beautiful. And like Steve, his cock reflected the rest of him. Julian had length but was slim.

They liked variety. But so did I, and I was very happy with the variety on offer tonight. "So how are we doing this?"

Julian smiled and patted the table. "One at each end, if you're happy being in the middle."

Not having to choose which one of them to have first suited me just fine. I walked over to the table, Steve following behind, and found that there were two damask napkins to go with the tablecloth, one at each end. The one closest to me was folded into a simple triangle, and the one further away was a more complex rolled and tucked affair. "You like a bit of formality, even for Friday night takeaway?"

Julian waved a hand at the table. "We do like the finer things in life." He smiled ruefully. "At least at the weekend when we've got time to appreciate them."

Upper class, but definitely no twit, and quite capable of sending himself up. I liked him even on a few minutes' acquaintance. Enough that I wanted more than just his cock. I took the extra few steps to stand in front of him and reach up to pull his head down for a kiss.

No taste of coffee here. Just the human taste of a warm mouth—and the feel of warm hands on the bare skin of my back as he pulled me closer. Then a body at my back as Steve hugged me from behind. Hugged both of us, and Julian pulled away, laughing.

"Damn it, two pairs of cold hands are a bit much!"

"Foreplay's off the menu, then?" I asked.

"Straight to the main course," Julian agreed.

Which would be me. I lifted myself up to sit on the edge of the table and carefully lowered myself back to lie flat. The folded napkin at the other end was in just the right place to let me hang my head back over the edge of the table in comfort.

For a moment, I had an upside-down view of the city below, the lights glimmering through the falling snow. Then Julian moved to stand in front of me so that all I cared about was the cock right in front of my eyes.

He had a thin condom on, thin enough that I could see every detail of the flesh beneath. I should have thought about that before, about fucking two strangers who fucked other strangers, but didn't feel the need now to check on Steve as well. I could hear the familiar rip of foil from where I lay.

I felt Steve's hands on my legs, pulling them wide apart. "Okay?" he asked.

"Go for it."

Steve did. Not Julian, not yet. Just that cock swaying tantalisingly in front of my mouth as Steve's cock pushed into me, opening me up. Slowly at first, giving me a chance to get used to it.

And then it felt right, and there was just the pleasure of a man inside me, making me want to thrust back against him. I couldn't in this position, not much, but maybe that was the point.

Sweet relief as Julian finally brought his cock within my reach, holding the shaft and tracing the head over my lips. I reached back to grab for it. Julian laughed, and said, "No biting."

"I won't. Not if you don't make me wait."

"Greedy."

Yes, I was greedy. I wanted both of them—wanted them filling me up.

"Open wide," Julian said, and I did. The position was perfect, and his cock slid smoothly into my mouth. A tiny pause, and then further in, giving me as much as I could take, as much as I could possibly want. And before I could feel that I needed to breathe, he pulled back, just enough to make me comfortable.

"All right?" he asked, and his voice wasn't quite so steady now. I gave him a thumbs-up sign.

With that, they both thrust into me, making me giddy with sensation. All I had to do was lie back and take it, a man at each end. Either alone would have been enough, but both together was overwhelming. Steve stretching me with each stroke, his size making it only just this side of being too much. Julian filling my mouth, my throat, making me very glad that I had my head tipped back over the edge of the table. Perfectly positioned for their pleasure and mine.

The only way it could have been better was if there'd been someone to suck my cock. But wishing for that would be just plain greedy when I already had more than enough for my needs. My own hand would do well enough.

As they thrust into me, I stroked my cock. A loose grip at first, needing something, but trying not to come too fast. Each thrust brought me that bit closer to the edge. Nothing fancy in it, just honest hard fucking, but I didn't need fancy. All I needed was what I already had—letting two strangers fuck me like this. Warm bodies in a warm flat, while only a few metres away the snow swirled through the air.

They thrust faster, obviously close to coming. I tightened my grip, keeping in time with them. But not quite in time, because Julian's smooth rhythm stuttered slightly, and then he shoved deep into my mouth and came.

Not so slim now, that cock, not when I wanted to breathe. Needed to breathe by the time he pulled out. But even so, I wanted him back in my mouth, wanted to feel them both in me as I came.

And then that thought was banished as Steve gripped his hand around mine and worked my cock with both our hands. "Go on, come for us," I heard one of them say and wasn't sure which of them it was. All I was sure of was that I could come for them, would come with one more stroke.

Steve gave it to me. And then I was coming, my own hot come splattering across my body where it was still damp from the coffee.

So much better than going home to that warm but empty flat of my own. It was still my own hand around my cock, but it was someone else's cock in my arse, someone else's hands warm on my bare shoulders. I lay back and enjoyed every last bit of sensation, from the glorious feel of coming, right down to the delicate texture of the damask tablecloth that lay between me and the table.

Steve was just far enough behind me that I could still feel the pulse of his orgasm inside me as I finished my own. He held still for a moment and then pulled out, dropping to his knees and laying his head on me for a moment.

Julian asked me, "Do you need some help getting up?"

"Actually, now you mention it..."

He shifted his grip on my shoulders, lifting me just enough that I could make it the rest of the way to a sitting position. Steve put a hand on the table and levered himself to his feet, moving back just enough to be out of my way as I eased off the table. He was grinning.

"Enjoy that?" he asked.

"Definitely worth getting soaked for." I looked down at myself. "Both times."

He laughed. "I think we'd both better go and have a shower, and not just for after-sex cleanup."

Coffee and come wasn't so bad a mix, but a hot shower still sounded wonderful. "Lead the way."

It was a fairly decent-sized walk-in shower, as befitted an expensive flat. Big enough for two if they were good friends. Definitely not big enough for three, though. "What about Julian?"

"There's another shower for the other bedroom, and he needs less cleaning up than we do." Steve smirked. "Besides, I did the shopping; he can get the food ready."

An equitable division of labour, had Steve actually had to put any effort into doing his shopping. On the other hand, Steve and I had paid upfront in wet discomfort for our evening's pleasure. It felt so good as the hot water hit my skin, taking away the last of any chill from the snow. Felt even better as Steve picked up a flannel and scrubbed my chest. Not seduction, just a gesture of hospitality. The sensual pleasure was in the heat, and feeling clean, and enjoying someone caring for me. "Thanks."

"You can do me next. But you needed it more; you got hit by most of the coffee."

"I suppose we could have had a shower first to warm up…"

"But we didn't want to wait."

No. It had been only a few minutes from Julian's accidental offer to the actual sex. Might almost as well have been round the back of a pub. But round the back of a pub wouldn't have had this afterwards—the lazy luxurious shower and dinner overlooking the city below.

We wallowed in the hot water for rather longer than was strictly needed to get clean. And when we got out, there were big, fluffy towels on a heated towel rail. Wouldn't have had that round the back of the pub, either.

The final touch was a dressing gown that felt warm and soft against my skin. As I wrapped it around me, Steve asked, "Better than waiting on the platform for a late tram?"

"*Much* better."

"And I promised you a hot drink as well."

We found Julian in the kitchen. "There's shepherd's pie. Or if that doesn't suit, we can send out for takeaway." He looked slightly embarrassed. "Food, I mean…"

"Shepherd's pie will be fine, thanks."

A few minutes later, I was sitting with Steve on a sofa, sipping my coffee and watching the snow fall. "This is a much better evening than I'd expected."

"Do you want to stay tonight? There's a spare bedroom."

Of course I did, with or without more sex. "Love to."

His smile made it clear that the offer had been genuine. His tone was teasing as he said, "At least your clothes should have dried out by morning."

"That's *not* the only reason I'm staying." I stretched out my legs and leaned back. "Nor is the sex, if I'm honest."

He nodded. "Nice just to stay in with company in this weather." Then he grinned. "Although I hope the sex is a factor."

I leaned over and kissed him. "You know damn well that it was good. And I'd be happy to have a second helping later."

"Good," said Julian from behind us. "Incidentally, is it my imagination, or did you two already know each other?"

We explained. That led into conversation about where we worked, which carried on as we sat down to dinner. The table was covered with the same spread of damask, although now it was set rather more conventionally. The food was good, and as we finished dessert I said so. Julian fairly glowed with pleasure, so I could guess who the cooking hobbyist was. "You obviously like a variety of sensual experiences."

He raised a glass of wine to me. "I have the great good fortune to have youth, health, and money. I am damn well going to make the most of the privilege."

And for this one night, I was invited to share in that. "Shall we clear the table?"

"For another round?" Steve asked. He glanced at Julian. "I don't mind the table again, but I'd like to go for my own fantasy, and there's something about the snow at night..." He sounded wistful.

Julian laughed softly and reached over to lay a hand on Steve's cheek. "I've had my turn, love. It's your turn now."

They smiled at each other, and for a moment, I was excluded; I might be inside the warm cocoon of their flat, but I was outside the very obvious love between them. Then Steve stood up and said, "We should clear the table since Julian set it."

When we'd finished, we went back through to the lounge. Once again, Julian was lit only by the city lights. But this time, he was lying on a chaise longue. His dressing gown had fallen open—or perhaps had been artfully posed. He was lounging back on a pile of cushions and had one arm draped along the backrest of the chaise, looking like something out of a Victorian erotic postcard—the sort that a Victorian gentleman could just about get away with claiming was Art, and therefore respectable— at least if he *were* a gentleman. Like Julian, in fact.

Steve was right. The swirling snow outside the window added to the scene, giving it a dreamlike quality. I was more than willing to go along with their dream, ride their fantasy with them. Whatever it was.

Steve slipped my dressing gown back over my shoulders so that it dropped to the floor. Then I walked over to stand by Julian, looking down at him. He was holding his cock now, working it slowly with his hand. Watching me and Steve standing behind me.

I couldn't guess at what it was they wanted of me. Easiest just to ask. "What do you want me to do?"

Steve ran his hand down my back, finishing with his finger resting just over my hole. He pushed it in just as he said, "Sit on his cock. Just sit."

Julian shifted down the chaise so that he was lying with his back still on the cushions, but his legs over the edge, with his feet firmly planted on the floor. In that position, it would be easy enough to stand over him and lower myself down. As I went to do so, Steve said, "No, facing the other way. So you can lie back against him."

I'd be lying on my back on top of Julian, giving Steve a perfect view of Julian's cock up my arse. Just like the less discreet sort of Victorian naughty postcard. Maybe that really was Steve's kink, and not just my idle fancy.

Steve obviously liked to watch, so I took it slowly, standing over Julian, and then easing myself down onto his cock. After the fucking Steve had given me earlier, I could have easily taken it in one go, but tantalising all three of us was more fun.

Finally I had it all in, and I leaned back against Julian. I had a good view as Steve knelt between Julian's legs. Steve took hold of my cock and licked the bottom of the shaft. That felt good, but it wasn't enough. Then Steve moved down—to suck my balls. First one, then the other, massaging them with his tongue.

I squirmed, trying to find a position where I could rock myself on Julian's cock, but Julian held me firm with an arm across my chest. "Wait," he said in my ear. I didn't have much choice because there was a wiry strength in that lean body. But relaxing was impossible while Steve's mouth worked its magic on my balls.

Steve moved lower still, leaving my balls alone. Then Julian gasped and dug his fingers into me, and I realised what Steve was doing—licking Julian's cock where it entered my body.

The image in my mind made me want to grab, to hold, to thrust. But Julian still held me, and I followed his lead, lying quiet for Steve to do as he willed. I was right at the edge of my self-control when Steve finally sat back a little and reached for something in the pocket of the dressing gown he still wore.

A tube of lube and a small vibrator.

It was a stretch going in, but the good sort of stretch that makes you certain you could manage a little more. Then Steve turned the vibrator on.

It would have been fantastic by itself. Jammed in alongside Julian's cock, it was mind-blowing. And that was before Steve started slowly moving it round from one side of Julian's cock to the other, sending sensation shooting through me.

Not just my arse, either. Julian was nuzzling at my neck and rolling one of my nipples between his fingertips. Enough of this and I'd come anyway, whether or not I was held too tightly to move.

Steve looked at us and grinned. "He's close enough."

"So am I," Julian said. "Get on with it."

Steve pulled out the vibrator, and I moaned. Julian said, "Patience. You'll be satisfied soon enough." He opened his legs a little more, spreading me wide.

And Steve leaned forward and pushed his cock into me.

Not all the way, although in the first shock, it felt like it. I yelped from surprise as much as pain. But he'd paused only an inch or two in and waited, watching me.

Julian asked, "Too much?"

Oh god. Both of them stuffed up me. It would be too much; it had to be too much. But I was already recovering from the shock, my arse greedy for more. "I can take it, if you're careful."

"I'll be careful," Steve promised. "Slow's better anyway."

He pushed in a little further and then back out. I could feel him doing something and then wet slickness. He must have put more lube on. I breathed hard and fast, trying to relax the right muscles. Back in, and his cock slipped in a little further this time. Julian gasped and pinched my nipple hard. Not deliberate, not this time.

Another stroke, wedging me open a little more. And again, and he must have had at least half his length into me by now. I kept thinking it must be all in and then realising that I could feel just Julian deep inside me, a shocking contrast to the thickness of both of them together.

A little more, and a little more. And then Steve really was all the way inside me, his cock alongside Julian's, both of them filling me to capacity.

Steve paused, somehow, giving me a moment to get used to it. And then he started thrusting in earnest, pulling back and sliding in again in a smooth, practiced rhythm.

Finally Julian let go of me, letting me move. Not that I needed to now. The strength of Steve's stroke pushed me back a little along Julian's cock and then let me slip forward again. Julian grabbed at my hips and pulled me back and forth, setting the pace he obviously liked.

Two cocks inside me—one long, one thick. Good thing I'd already been thoroughly fucked once tonight. I was open enough to take them both, but we'd had a long enough break over dinner that I was going to come quickly. So were they, going by the look on Steve's face, and the way Julian's breathing was harsh and quick in my ear.

Might as well go for broke. "Harder!"

And they did, slamming into me. Not quite in rhythm for one stroke, and then two. On the third, they fucked me together, both cocks jammed right up inside me, and I came.

I was overloaded with sensation, couldn't think about anything except the way it felt. Didn't even notice whether they were still going. For a very long moment, it was about nothing but me.

When I finally started to come down, they'd also come. They held position for another moment or two before Steve slowly eased out of me.

First one cock gone, and then the other, leaving me empty. Empty, but satisfied. Julian held me a moment or two longer before saying, "Help us up, love."

Steve pulled himself to his feet and then held out a hand to me. I felt stiff as I staggered to my feet, and I knew I'd ache in the morning, but it had been well worth it. Steve helped Julian up before turning back to me. "Have I apologised adequately for spilling my coffee over you?"

"More than adequately." But I didn't want it to end there. They'd implied that Friday nights were random pickups, never the same twice. Would they consider more than once with me? "Do you two have a set menu, or do you like to experiment?"

Steve flicked a glance behind me at Julian. Then he smiled and said, "Oh, I think we have a few more flavour combinations we should work through. We can draw up a new menu in the morning."

It turned out that, between us, we had quite an extensive list of things we wouldn't mind trying at least once. We drew up that menu four months ago, and Friday nights haven't been the same for me since. It's usually a starter by Julian, dessert by Steve, and a lazy Saturday morning breakfast in bed by me, although Julian always cooks dinner for us. So working through the permutations could take us a while yet. And summer's coming up, with the prospect of balmy Friday nights and dinner on the balcony. Though we'll probably have to close the blinds if things get too hot…

Management

Practices

"FUCKING CHAMPAGNE SOCIALIST!" Guy snapped. "Although I suppose I should be grateful you are; at least you're not suggesting we move out of the hotel and into accommodation more like that of the labour force."

Tristan glowered at him. "I can't help being born with a silver spoon in my mouth. That doesn't mean I can't care about the conditions the people working for me are working under."

"So they still believe in teaching good old-fashioned social responsibility at that posh school you went to?" Probably wasn't the only good old-fashioned thing they taught, but it didn't seem appropriate to bring that up with a colleague. Although it was difficult not to think about it—not when he'd had the pleasure of viewing Tristan in the shower block on-site. "We were sent here as site engineers, remember, not bloody union recruiters. I've had enough of this. I'll see you at breakfast." He made to leave, intending to go back to his own room.

Tristan grabbed him and shoved him up against the wall, leaning against him to make sure he couldn't get away. Since Tristan had several inches on him and was built like the varsity rugby player Tristan had in fact been, this was a fairly effective, and unfair, way of continuing the conversation. It was also damned distracting, given his taste for large men with sexy voices.

Attack seemed the best form of defence. "So you're all for workers having control as long as they agree with you?"

"*You're* an equal."

"But you're in charge. Besides, I didn't go to a posh school like yours. I had to learn how to stand up to intimidation somewhere a bit rougher." Oh hell, Tristan this close, when they were both on an adrenaline rush, was having an effect. "And I don't suppose you were on the bottom even at school?"

Talk about Freudian slips.

Tristan looked even more pissed off. "Did it ever occur to you that I might have reason to dislike abuse of power?" He shoved against Guy. "I've been on the receiving end." Then his eyes widened slightly. "You like it rough."

By the feel of things, so did Tristan. Was it worth the risk to their professional relationship? Or the stormy but real friendship they'd built up? Yes. It was.

"Not usually. Occasionally I quite enjoy it with someone I can trust."

Tristan's expression changed—still angry, but something else laid over it. Now what?

Oh—he'd implied he trusted Tristan sexually.

"Guy…" Tristan trailed off, seemed to think about it, and then said, "I always assumed you'd think I was bullying you."

"I know you better than that. You might ride roughshod over me half the time, but only until I yell at you that you are."

"Are you sure?"

"No. But we've just destroyed any illusion of a pure and chaste relationship."

Tristan nodded once and then shoved him towards the bed. He fought back, carefully. Not that he was fighting just for show, but it would be rather unsporting to resort to the more vicious moves he'd learnt in self-defence classes. He had, after all, more or less invited Tristan to do this.

Tristan's greater weight and strength told in the end. Guy found himself flat on his back on the bed, Tristan's weight pinning him down, Tristan's cock hard against his. He twisted against Tristan, testing his strength, unable to break free. Tristan's face was flushed with arousal, still tinged with an exciting edge of anger.

"You aren't going anywhere until I've finished with you, Guy."

He swung his hand towards Tristan's face, open-palmed rather than risking a fist. Tristan caught his wrist, forced it back against the bed. Before he could try with the other hand, Tristan had grabbed that wrist as well. He was trapped, his body pinned by Tristan's, his wrists held in a grip of iron. Then Tristan ground against his cock, a slow, merciless torture that sent a thrill cascading through his nervous system. He moaned in pleasure, and Tristan grinned savagely.

"Not quite as detached as you like to play at?"

Another roll of Tristan's hips, and then Tristan's mouth came down on his. Tristan was too wary to try a full kiss, but even the heavy pressure of his lips was enough to make Guy moan again. Tristan pulled away and let go of one wrist, reaching for Guy's throat and the top button of his shirt.

Guy promptly hit him.

"You little bastard!" Tristan grabbed his wrist again, forced it back. This time it hurt, and badly. He'd ended up with his arm over the edge of the bed, and Tristan was forcing it down, forcing it too far. He yelped in pain.

Tristan let go instantly, the anger vanishing, replaced by concern. "Shit, I didn't realise... Are you all right?"

He flexed his hand. The arm felt a little sore, but otherwise undamaged. He nodded.

"Want to go on?"

He could trust Tristan. Trust Tristan not to stop before he'd reached his limits, trust him not to push past those limits.

"Yes."

Tristan leaned down, kissed him again. As he tried to turn away, Tristan seized his free wrist. *Damn.*

Tristan pulled on his wrists, stretching his arms above his head. Short of headbutting Tristan or kicking him, he had nothing left to try. Kicking him wasn't likely to be that successful, anyway. He lay still, staring up into Tristan's face. "Bastard."

"Pleasant as it would be to shut you up temporarily, I don't have anything handy to wedge between your teeth. So I'll have your arse. That end doesn't bite."

"Try it," he snarled.

"I'll do more than try it," Tristan said. "I'm going to fuck you so hard you won't be able to sit down for a week."

He thrust involuntarily at that. Tristan chuckled.

"Like the idea?"

"Get off me!"

"Oh, I intend to. Just long enough to get your trousers off." Tristan suddenly moved, dragging their arms down. Taken by surprise, Guy didn't resist in time, and as he tried to twist away, Tristan tucked his hands beneath the small of his back, grabbed both wrists in one hand, and leaned hard on him, trapping his arms with his own weight. "And then I'll decide whether I want you from the front or the back. To begin with, at any rate." Tristan slid his free hand between them and groped for the fastenings of Guy's trousers. Since Tristan couldn't lift his weight off Guy without risking him getting loose, it involved a lot of fumbling. Even through his trousers, it felt good.

Then Tristan found the tag of the zip, pulled it down, and slid a hand inside. "Silk underwear. Very nice. You are decadent, aren't you?"

"You, of course, would rather be a man of the people, even to their clothing." Tristan's hand on his cock, sliding a little on the silk, made it hard to think of a suitably cutting reply. He'd fancied Tristan for a long time, fantasised about that burly body pinning him down, that deep voice murmuring obscenities in his ear. Having it happening in reality seemed to have switched off his brain.

"I think you'd do better without any clothing at all." More fumbling, as the underwear was dragged over his cock. Then Tristan pulled his hand out and placed it over Guy's mouth, the index finger resting on his lips. "Lick it."

"No." The feel of his lips brushing over Tristan's finger as he spoke made him want to do more than lick it. He wanted to draw it in, suck on it. But he wasn't submitting, not yet.

"You want it up your arse dry? Or perhaps you want my cock up there dry without even a finger first?"

"That would hurt you as well."

Tristan smiled at him. Not a nice smile. "Oh, but not as much as it would hurt you. It might be worth it." A hard thrust against his groin, and he groaned, quite unable to stop himself. "On the other hand, you'd probably only enjoy it." Another thrust, the rough fabric of Tristan's trousers scraping against his cock as Tristan moved. "Want it dry? I'll be quite willing to oblige you. After all, I can always make you kiss my cock better afterwards if it gets rubbed too hard by a nice tight arse."

Right on one of his secret fantasies. Tristan tearing his clothes off, shoving straight into him, no preliminaries. He was too damned sensible to ever try it, given the size of Tristan's cock, but that didn't stop his own cock responding to the idea when it was described to him by Tristan, with those wonderfully sexy undertones vibrating through Tristan's voice. He was close to coming, one good hard shove up his arse and he'd be gone.

"Lick it," Tristan repeated, and he obeyed without thinking. "Thank you," Tristan said and took his hand away, just before Guy succumbed to the desire generated by Tristan's words and started sucking on his finger. Then Tristan slid his hand between them again and brushed his wet fingertip over the tip of Guy's cock.

You cheat! was Guy's last indignant thought before orgasm deprived him of the ability to think at all.

Somewhere in the burst of pleasure, he noticed that Tristan was kissing him again, and this time thoroughly, tongue ravaging his mouth. Arms tight around him, still holding his wrists behind him, one wrist in each hand again. Completely possessed. He couldn't move, didn't want to move.

As it faded, Tristan let go, moved off him. He slumped back in a sated sprawl, too exhausted to move more than the necessary amount to free his arms from behind his back. Tristan had vanished, which peeved him a little, but only a little. He closed his eyes and floated in a pleasant haze.

His doze was interrupted by someone handling his feet. He registered it as his shoes and socks being removed and ignored it. It was very convenient to have someone else undress him, rather than having to do it himself. Then his trousers were pulled off, and his underwear.

"Do you have any idea what you look like?" Tristan said.

He opened his eyes, looked up to find Tristan standing near the bed.

"Sprawled there half naked, with all your...assets on display." Tristan's gaze moved down his body, stopped at his cock. "Available." Tristan licked his lips, and Guy shivered. He'd never thought of Tristan as...lustful, was the best word he could think of.

"Perhaps not all your assets. Sit up a little."

He propped a couple of pillows against the wall, in the corner, and leaned back on them. Tristan came closer and pulled his knees apart. He let himself be handled into position, no fighting now. Tristan arranged him and then stepped back, leaving him half sitting, half lying on the pillows, with his feet together and his knees spread, a pose that let him lay comfortably while leaving him completely exposed, cock, balls, and hole. He was property on display. His cock twitched at the thought.

"Very pretty," Tristan said. "I still haven't decided whether to take you from the front or the back first. I think I'll just leave you like that until I've prepared myself."

Tristan put his hand on his fly and pulled down the zip slowly, his gaze never leaving Guy. Very deliberate movement indeed; that and the proprietorial expression on Tristan's face focusing Guy's attention on the fact that Tristan intended to have him regardless of his own opinion on the matter. Would enjoy him fighting back, since he wouldn't be able to match Tristan's strength, and there was no chance of him getting away. The surge of pleasure at the idea nicely overrode the sensible part of his mind that told him Tristan would stop if convinced his objection was genuine. Tristan's hot gaze on his body, taking ownership without so much as laying a finger on him, was enough to make his own cock lift even before Tristan's emerged.

And what a cock—long and thick and hard, gleaming as Tristan spread oil on it with an easy motion, hand slicking up and down, working himself but never once looking down at his own cock. Always looking at Guy.

Finally, Tristan took his hand away, giving Guy a clear view of Tristan's cock as it jutted from his open trousers. Big and beautiful, and Guy started to wonder whether Tristan had been serious about shoving it up him without oiling his arse first. He wasn't quite certain whether to be delighted or appalled by the idea. He was well out of practice and that was rather a lot of cock even if it was oiled.

Then Tristan stepped towards the bed, still holding the pot of lubricant. "Tempting though the idea of taking you dry is, I'd rather be certain I'm in a fit state to fuck you twice if I feel like it. It would be a pity to *have* to use your mouth the second time." Tristan sat on the edge of the bed and dipped his fingers into the pot. "Try to kick me, and you'll regret it."

Guy checked his movement. The position he was in didn't allow for a sudden strike, and he had no doubt whatsoever that if he really hurt Tristan, without actually disabling him, Tristan would instantly make him regret it. Besides, kicking wasn't anywhere near as much fun as wrestling. He settled for edging back as Tristan touched his arse. Tristan didn't try to follow, simply grabbed his balls with the other hand.

"Sit still."

He sat. Tristan shoved a finger into him, and he gasped at the sudden pain. Not very much pain—just enough to put an edge on his pleasure.

"I see you would have liked it dry," Tristan said and pushed the finger all the way in. "Perhaps another time." The finger moved inside him, circling. "There *will* be another time, I assure you." Tristan withdrew slightly and then forced another finger in, grinning as Guy jumped and then winced at the pain caused by his sudden movement. "I don't suppose this is a permanent surrender. It will be fun breaking you again, for however many times I have to do it before you do give in."

"Fuck off."

"Oh, at least one more finger before I do that. You're so bloody tight that I think you'll need three."

In fact, one finger would have been enough, even with a cock the size of Tristan's, but he had no intention of saying so. He was enjoying it far too much as foreplay to forego it, and he appreciated the way Tristan was making absolutely certain he'd be all right without breaking the scene to ask him.

Tristan added the third finger, stretching him, the other hand still gently squeezing his balls. "I don't really want to have to haul you down to Casualty—it would be rather embarrassing to have to explain how I found you, say, indulging yourself with an oversized sex toy."

Guy managed to tear his fascinated gaze away from Tristan's face long enough to glance down at Tristan's cock. It was quite true; he *was* indulging himself with an oversized sex toy.

Tristan noticed where he was looking. "Yes, it is rather big. Perhaps four, just to be on the safe side. Besides, I'm enjoying this. You're so pretty when you're all dishevelled and trying not to enjoy the feel of a man controlling you."

Four fingers inside him. Four *big* fingers. It felt wonderful, and he wanted more. It surprised him just what he wanted. It had been a long time since he'd trusted someone enough for that.

Tristan withdrew his fingers. "No, I think I will have you from the front after all. You look so...vulnerable, like that."

"No."

"Not your choice, Guy."

"No. I don't want that."

Tristan looked at him. There had been a last remaining trace of real anger firing the lust. Now the anger had returned. "What do you mean, no? Now? You've had yours, but I don't get mine?"

He reached down, took Tristan's hand in his, and lifted it up. Then he closed Tristan's fingers into a fist.

He saw in Tristan's eyes the exact moment when it dawned on Tristan what he was offering, what he was asking for. The anger was suddenly replaced by shock. Then a slowly creeping tenderness, and...fear?

"No, Guy. I can't."

"Why not?" This wasn't what he'd expected.

"I could hurt you. For real." Tristan freed his hand, curled it about Guy's. "I won't risk it."

"Not if you're careful. And there's always the hotel nurse, in case of accident."

"Not this time," Tristan said firmly. "Another time, when we're more used to each other. When I know you better, know how you'll react. I'd rather wait."

He hadn't expected to be turned down. It simply hadn't occurred to him that Tristan would refuse, not when Tristan so evidently enjoyed rough sex. "You may be waiting a long time," he warned. "I meant what I said about this being an occasional pleasure. I'm not often in the mood for fisting."

"I'll wait."

Tristan wasn't going to budge, that much was obvious. And even if Guy had been inclined to rape, getting someone's fist inside him was one activity that did rather require the active co-operation of the other person. He'd have to settle for cock.

"All right. If you won't... Where were we?"

"I was going to have you from the front. But I've changed my mind. I don't think you're really quite submissive enough for my taste yet. On your knees."

"Make me." He bared his teeth, glad Tristan had so easily restored the mood.

"With pleasure." Tristan stood up and then seized his ankles with crossed arms, pulled his legs straight and twisted one ankle over the other in one fluid movement. He could roll over, or he could have his ankle joints sprained. He rolled over. Tristan was on him before he could recover—a hot weight on his back. "I could take you now," Tristan said, "but I really would rather have you on your knees."

"In your dreams."

"My wet dreams," Tristan said and shifted, sitting up and leaning his hands on Guy's shoulder blades, fingertips digging in. Then he slid backwards to sit on Guy's calves, always holding Guy down, his hands running down Guy's back. Then hands on Guy's hips, pulling at him. Guy tried to resist, fingers digging into the mattress to find purchase, but Tristan was stronger. He was pulled to his knees, held there. Finally he stopped trying to fight free.

"Good boy," Tristan crooned and twisted his hands, gripping the side of Guy's hips with his fingers and using his thumbs to spread Guy's buttocks a little. Guy shivered, but held still, and was rewarded with

Tristan's hands moving across his arse, holding him wide open to Tristan's view.

"Oh, very nice." As Guy tried to move up onto all fours, he said, "No, don't move, keep your head down. I want you stretched wide like this."

He froze in place, waiting as Tristan looked at him. Tristan's fingers digging into him a little, not enough to hurt, just enough to remind him that he was held. And then bliss as Tristan's weight shifted on his calves, and he felt Tristan's cock up against him, into him, deep inside him in one easy glide. Then Tristan held still; they both held still, for one long breath, before Tristan pulled back again, nearly all the way. The next thrust wasn't a thrust, but Tristan pulling him by the hips, pulling him back onto that wonderful length of flesh.

"Shouldn't have"—Tristan gasped and thrust again—"given you that last finger after all." Another thrust, and he shoved back to meet it. "Tight enough for me"—he squeezed down on Tristan, hard, and Tristan gasped before going on—"but it could have been tighter, and you'd still have taken it." A hand groped for his cock. "Wouldn't you?"

"Yes," he moaned, balanced between the cock up his arse and the hand on his own cock, wanting to move in both directions at once. Then Tristan solved his dilemma by taking the hand away, laying it on his hip again.

"Brace yourself against the bed," Tristan ordered, and he did so, wondering why. Then Tristan was pulling his cheeks apart again, hands rough on his flesh. "Only a little deeper this way, but I'm sure you'll appreciate it." And he thrust again.

He did appreciate it. Deeply. Tristan's belly right up against him, the full length in him, balls bouncing heavily against him. Then Tristan's voice seducing him again.

"I want to feel you tighter than that when I come. I want you squeezing me. You'll come when I tell you to and not before."

If Tristan didn't stop rotating his hips very gently, or at least shut up, it was going to be very difficult to wait long enough to obey that order.

"Now, Guy."

To his surprise, he did. He hadn't *really* thought Tristan could bring him to orgasm just by talking to him. And then he couldn't think at all, was simply a bundle of reactions, pouring come onto the bedclothes, aware of nothing but how *good* it felt. Then he was done, collapsing onto the bed, Tristan following him down to sprawl on top of him.

They lay like that for a few minutes, and then Tristan pulled out of him and slid off to lie next to him. He managed to crack an eye open and examined Tristan's face. Tristan's postorgasmic expression was rather appealing. As if the man had finally forgotten the devils that were driving him, if only for a little while. Perhaps they should do this more often. Or at least again. Again tonight wasn't really an option, though, not for him.

Tristan had apparently noticed he had an audience. "Oh, you're awake? I obviously didn't do it hard enough the first time."

He grinned. "Were you planning on finishing the job?"

"In a few minutes."

"Just how long *is* your refractory period?"

"Longer than yours. But I haven't had sex for a while."

Neither have I. "Are you implying that I suffer from satyrism?"

"No." Tristan looked interested. "Do you?"

"No. If you want another round, I'm not going to stop you, but I can't promise to be as enthusiastic."

"And here I was looking forward to forcing you. It's no fun if you just lie there."

So Tristan really did enjoy him fighting back. "Sorry, Tristan." He rolled onto his back. "Too tired to play."

Tristan propped himself up on one elbow and leaned over him. "You are too, aren't you? Do you mind if I...?"

He'd had two, and Tristan had had only one. He spread his legs a little. "As long as you don't mind me lying back and thinking of England."

Tristan laughed at him. "I'd rather you lie back and think of the glorious workers' revolution."

He shuddered. "Thank you, but no. There are limits to my masochism."

Tristan only grinned and shuffled to the edge of the bed, standing up to undress. Guy enjoyed the view, admiring Tristan's body without feeling any urge to get up and jump on it. Perhaps tomorrow.

Tristan was back on him, not bothering with foreplay, for which Guy was duly grateful. He was quite willing to offer a hole for Tristan's use, but that didn't mean he should be expected to pretend an interest in proceedings when he was beyond interest in anything other than the opportunity for a cuddle. Tristan seemed quite happy to offer him that, at least, holding him, kissing him gently before saying, "Lift your legs."

He obliged Tristan, it being easier to do so than argue about turning over and just lying there. Besides, he liked being able to hold Tristan back.

Tristan performed efficiently and quickly, and it was over within a minute or two. Another few minutes of lying under Tristan's weight, and then Tristan rose to his knees, starting to undo Guy's shirt.

"What are you, my valet?"

"You'd love that, wouldn't you? No, just getting you ready for bed. I think you need a shower after that."

"Don't want a shower."

Tristan pulled at his shoulders until he sat up, and then he pulled the shirt off him. "You're sweaty and sticky and dirty, and so am I. Come on, get up." He was lifted, very reluctantly on his part, until he was standing.

"Wait until the morning."

Tristan half carried, half dragged him into the shower. "Don't argue with me, Guy. You need cleaning up. You'll regret it in the morning if you don't."

"Too tired," he mumbled in reply. All he wanted to do was sleep, but the practical part of his mind agreed with Tristan. He'd regret it in the morning if he didn't clean up now.

"Then I'll do it for you." Tristan did so, holding Guy against him, soaping them both with an attention to detail that Guy would have found very pleasant a little earlier. He made a mental note to ask for a replay at some future time when he could appreciate it properly. Rinsed, turned around, process repeated on his front. He had to make some effort to support himself for this, not just slump against Tristan, and was relieved when it was over. Out of the shower and a brisk towel dry before they returned to the bedroom.

He reached for his clothes, only to be interrupted by Tristan saying, "Stay. Please?"

What the hell? It was a queen-sized bed, quite big enough for one large and one medium-sized engineer to share. He climbed into bed.

Tristan climbed in with him. "So, we're still partners?"

"Work, sex, and play. Now can I go to sleep?"

"Goodnight, Guy. We do still have to go to work in the morning."

Another month of it. Still, it promised to be a more interesting project than they'd worked on together before.

CAR WASH

IT'S NOT CHEAP being a uni student, even if you live frugally. I did my best with bar work, but during term there's a limit to how much time you can spend working a paying job, instead of studying, at least if you want good grades. My parents could afford to support me in comfort, but they were more likely to help out beyond the minimum if I showed a bit of effort on my own account. That's why I welcomed any chance of a bit of casual work during the summer vacation, however menial.

But there's one vacation job I'm not telling the aged parents about. I don't think they'd approve. Even if it did involve doing a good turn for a neighbour.

I was at home on my own for a couple of weeks, supposedly putting in some quality study time while Mum and Dad were away on a cruise. They'd offered to take me along, but I'd seen the brochure, and it didn't seem like my thing. Besides, I didn't want to cramp their style.

So I had the house to myself and plenty of quiet time, which I'd been making good use of for the first couple of days. But there's only so much studying a boy can do on a hot summer's day, and by lunchtime my brain was fried. I wanted a bit of exercise before going back to my books, and giving Dad's car a quick wash seemed like a good way to kill two birds with one stone—exercise, and being helpful. Even if I didn't do the full wash and wax routine, a quick hose down would be appreciated.

So there I was, stripped down to my shorts and the sun hot on my bare shoulders as I leaned over the bonnet, when a voice said from behind me, "I love physical work. I could watch it for hours."

Rod, one of the neighbours from the expensive end of the street. Same sort of age as my parents, but that hadn't stopped me wanting to watch him for hours last summer. Rod was well built, and well hung. Or, at least, there was enough bulk in his trouser crotch to interest a boy who'd worked out that he liked boys as well as girls, but not whether he liked them even more than girls. I'd had a few fantasies about seeing whether that bulk was all Rod. And about getting my arse speared by it—being stretched wide by its thickness.

"When you've finished that, would you like to come and do mine?" Rod asked.

The usual sort of banter from passers-by, but it wasn't just banter. The other thing that I liked about Rod was his car. Rod had a lot of money, and he had no spouse, no kids, and no pets to spend it on. At least, no pet animals. What he did have was a pet Jaguar, of the vehicular kind. A couple of other classic cars as well, but the 1950s Jag was his beloved, his baby doll. All gleaming paintwork, polished wood, and soft leather, and I loved her too. She was a lady, and she knew it.

"There's twenty quid in it," Rod added. "I know it's more of a kid's pocket money job, but I expect you could do with some beer money now you're at uni. And maybe a beer as well, if this heat keeps up."

Twenty quid to fondle the Jag. Well, I wasn't going to get much studying done in this heat anyway. "Love to." I turned around. Rod was in T-shirt and shorts, looking every inch not the investment banker he was during the week. He looked pretty hot in the suit he wore when he was investment banking, but I liked the weekend outfit best. Like I said, well built, and I could see a lot more of that hot bod right now. "You know how much I like that car."

Couldn't see his eyes behind those expensive sunglasses, but his mouth curved in a smile. "Yeah. Anyone would think you were taking her out on a date, the way you talk to her."

He'd obviously heard me whispering sweet nothings to her when I'd earned that pocket money washing her over the last couple of summers. I grinned back. "Would have taken her out on a date, too, if her daddy had let me drive her around town." I'd never asked, because I knew what the answer would be. Would you let a kid, who'd just passed his test, take out your beloved classic car?

"Give it a couple of years, son. Maybe when you've finished your degree, I'll let you take her round the block." And to take out the sting, he added, "Because I can trust you to wait until you know she'll be safe with you."

"Okay. Give me a few minutes to finish what I'm doing."

"No hurry, son. Your parents are away, aren't they?" He nodded at Dad's car. "Finish that off and lock up, and then come round to my place. I'll be out the back with a couple of beers."

HE WAS ROUND the back, and so was the Jag. Big house, big garden, and still plenty of space for a gravel turning circle beside the garage. It was a lovely spot, sheltered and sunny, and completely private once I'd locked the side gate behind me. Rod liked sharing his toys, but only with the invited. He made sure that his baby doll was safe from vandals even when she was out sunbathing.

Rod was lying back on a sun lounger, a hat shading his face, but the rest of him in full sun. And rather more of him on display than there had been a few minutes ago. He'd stripped down to just the shorts and a pair of sandals, with his chest bare. Nothing I hadn't seen before, but it still made me stumble for a step, thinking about wanting to test how hard those muscles were, run my hands through the pelt on his chest.

It shouldn't hit me like this. I'd finally got myself fucked at university, and I knew what it was like to have cock fill my arse. Didn't have to fantasise about it. But the guys at uni had been other guys like me, young and horny and somehow not quite finished yet. Rod was something else—all man, and comfortable with it.

And was also a neighbour offering me a couple of hours' work, so I'd better put my tongue away and get on with it.

He waved a hand at the buckets and hose by the car. "It's all yours."

"Thanks for the job."

He gave me a lazy smile that made my blood race. "The pleasure's all mine. I do like watching someone else hard at work."

Was I imagining just the faintest emphasis on the "hard"?

But the car was waiting for me. I turned and walked over to her, stopping just long enough to run a hand over her sleek bonnet before bending down to check how clean her wheel arches were. She felt and looked fairly clean already, just needing a touch-up, rather than needing a good hose down to start with. So I picked up the sponge and started shampooing the roof panel. A small patch—then bending down to rinse the sponge and pick up fresh shampoo—then stretching to reach the centre of the panel. Feeling my own muscles flex as I leaned that little bit further.

It felt good to stretch with the sun hot on my back, the heat soothing away the last of the ache where I'd been bent over my books all morning. As I dropped the sponge in the bucket one last time, I put my hands in the small of my back and arched my spine, feeling everything untangle. Then I picked up the bucket and moved around to the other side of the car.

I glanced over the roof at Rod and saw that the bulge in his crotch was a lot bigger and straighter than I'd seen earlier.

Oh god.

And I'd been talking to Baby Doll again, not even consciously realising it until now. Rod had got hard watching me make love to his car. I ducked my head and focused very carefully on the patch of roof just in front of me, trying not to think about the bulge in my own shorts. Baby Doll was between me and her daddy, so at least he couldn't see how turned on I suddenly was.

It didn't help. Every time I stretched, I was aware of the way my body moved. Every time I bent down to rinse the sponge, I felt my cock shift, rubbing against my shorts. I badly wanted to rub it against something else, anything that would give me a bit more pressure. But best of all would be the matching hardness in Rod's shorts.

I didn't look up towards Rod until I had to move down to work on Baby Doll's bonnet. And Rod wasn't in the chair any more.

"Go on"—he said from behind me—"fuck her. Just make sure you don't scratch her paint work."

"*What?*"

"You're too inexperienced to handle her on the road." He cupped my arse with one hand. "But I don't think you're too inexperienced to know how to wank by rubbing against her." He laughed quietly. "Not after a year at university, out of sight of your parents."

Oh god. I'd fantasised about it, and well before I'd gone to university. Never dared do it. Not just scared of getting caught. Scared of damaging her, of scratching that gleaming paint with a misplaced button or zip.

"But drop your shorts first," Rod said, letting go of my arse. "You can keep your boxers on if you're shy, as long as they don't have anything that could scratch her."

I could fuck Baby Doll, if I let Rod watch me do it. My cock ached just thinking about it.

Without even realising I was doing it, I dropped the sponge and put my hands to my fly. Then I stopped.

Did I really want to do this? Wank out in the open where anyone could see me? And not just wanking, but doing it by thrusting against a *car*?

Except the hedges were high, the gate was locked, and nobody could see me except Rod, who already knew how I felt about Baby Doll. And probably knew how I felt about him.

Let's do it.

I undid my fly and let the shorts drop around my ankles. There wasn't anything on my boxers that could hurt Baby Doll, so I kept those on for now. A little bit out of, yes, shyness, but mostly since I thought that maybe Rod had said it because he wanted to see me like that.

I was standing so close to her that all I had to do was lean forward and lean my arms on the bonnet to support myself. Even through my boxers, her body was hot against mine. She'd been sitting in the sun, her skin soaking up the heat just as mine had. Hot and hard, and just what I needed as I thrust against her. Sun still hot on my back, reminding me that I was outdoors and that anyone could walk in—*if* Rod had given them the key to the gate.

But right here and now, there was only Rod to see me fuck that sleek body. I pictured it in my mind—Rod watching my arse rising and falling as I fucked his baby doll.

She was good; she was everything I'd dreamed, but this still wasn't enough. I wanted skin to skin, even if her skin was hard metal rather than soft flesh. I pulled off her for a second or two, just long enough to pull my boxers down over my hips. Then back against the car, frantic now for sensation. Still hot, but now my cock was sliding over the smooth metal. I knew what I must look like, shorts around my ankles, boxers held around my thighs by their elastic waistband, arse bare to the warm air. My hole on display each time I thrust against the car and pulled back again.

And then Rod slid his finger down between my buttocks, coming to rest right where you'd expect. He didn't push his finger inside me. No, I did that. All he had to do was keep his finger exactly where it was, and I thrust back onto it as I pulled back for another stroke against Baby Doll. It slipped easily inside me, surprising me. And then I realised that he must have used the soap on his finger first.

Fingers, because as I gasped and shoved forward and then back again, he gave me another. I was caught between the car and his fingers, rocking back and forth and getting fucked either way. Baby Doll hot and hard against me when I flung myself forward, Rod's fingers slipping inside me as I pulled back. He held still the first couple of times, letting me fuck myself on him, but when I didn't protest, he must have taken that for my consent. As I thrust forward against the car, he followed my motion, shoving his fingers deep inside me. Twisting and curling them so my mind nearly exploded as he kneaded me.

Before I could push back again, he planted his other hand between my shoulders and shoved one thigh up behind mine, not forcing my face right down against the bonnet, but still pinning me down. "You like that?"

"Oh god, Rod, please..."

"Ask me to stop, and I will."

And I believed him. If I asked him to stop, he would, and he might never, ever do it again. So if I wanted him to fuck me, I had to let him do it here and now, outside and up against Baby Doll. Any way he wanted. "Please..."

He leaned a little harder on my back, worked his fingers even deeper inside my arse. "Please, Rod, stop, or please, Rod, fuck me?"

I couldn't quite make myself say it. So I simply stopped resisting that hand between my shoulders and let him push me right down so that I was lying across Baby Doll's bonnet. I turned my head to one side so that I could rest my cheek against her sweet hide.

"Good boy," Rod said. "Hold still while I open you up. You're tighter than I expected."

I finally found my voice. "It's not my first time."

"Not even with a car?" He sounded amused.

I could feel my cheeks burn. "Okay, first time with a car. Or even on a car."

"So, I do get to claim one bit of your virginity." He slid another finger inside me. I'd have jumped, but he was still leaning on me, his weight pressing me down. "You're tight enough that you're going to need something to slick you up before I fuck you." He paused to let me think about that. He wasn't just bragging, either. I could feel his cock pressed against my hip, and even allowing for my overactive imagination, that was one hell of a big cock he was proposing to shove inside me. "I could just sponge you down. Or there's the cream wax I was going to get you to use when you'd finished washing her. I was looking forward to watching you cream her up, but you looked in need of a bit of service yourself."

I bucked and damn near creamed her without any outside assistance.

"I'll take that as a yes." He worked my hole hard for another couple of strokes and then pulled out. I was desperate to get those fingers back, but at least I could think again. If I could just hang on for another minute, I'd have all I wanted—Rod's cock stretching me wide open and his full weight forcing it in.

Rod stood up, taking his weight off me, but I stayed where I was, stretched out across Baby Doll for his pleasure. I tried to hold still, not thrust against her, afraid of coming too soon. Then Rod said, "Spread your cheeks."

I managed to get my hands out from under me, so that I could pull my arse cheeks apart for him. He didn't do anything much for a moment, just teasing my hole with the tip of his finger. Not even slicked up, so that I could feel the slight drag of skin on skin. "That's a pretty little hole you've got there. Don't worry. You're careful with my baby doll, so I'll be careful with you. I'm not going to tear anything."

Then one finger again, but this time slicked with more than soapy water. It was cool and smooth, but nowhere near enough to cool the fire burning in me. Nor was the second finger. I wanted more, but as I tried to thrust against Baby Doll, Rod pulled his fingers out of me. "Hold still."

I did as I was told. I wanted his cock, and if that meant holding still even when I was desperate for pressure on my own cock, well, I'd hold still.

I was rewarded with a hand around my balls. Only for a few seconds, but Rod knew just how hard to squeeze to make it feel good without making it impossible to hold on.

Sun hot on my back, metal hot under my cheek and my chest, the smell of freshly cleaned paint work right under my nose. A big, hot hand cupping my balls. This was my reward for getting out there and doing Dad's car—I got to do Rod's car—and Rod.

"Want it pretty badly, don't you?" He let go of my balls. "How badly do you want it?"

Badly enough not to care whether anyone was listening over the hedge. "Please, Rod. Fuck me." I could hear the whine in my voice and didn't care. I wanted cock, and I wanted it now.

"Then hold still, and keep your cheeks spread for me. I want to watch the way your hole eats my cock."

That made me pull my cheeks apart as wide as I could. Nothing happened for a second or two, and then I heard the sound of a condom packet being torn open. He was fast about putting the condom, and almost immediately I could feel the thick weight of his cock rest against me for a moment, the whole length of it laid along my skin. Then he pulled back, but only for a second. The next second there was something big and blunt resting right on my hole, and I was suddenly glad he'd taken that time to open me up a bit. He really was hung like a horse; there hadn't been anything but Rod under those shorts, and all of it was about to go right into my arse.

But not all at once. He pressed forward, just a little, and the head caught and then popped inside me, stretching my hole wide. But just the head, Rod holding it there. Then he pulled back a little, slowly. Not enough to make it pop out again, just enough for me to feel the way my hole was tight around the shaft behind the head.

"Damn, but I like the look of that," Rod said. "I should have brought my camera out, so I could show you how much your arse likes sucking on my cock."

Jesus. I didn't want to be on camera, maybe to be shared around. But I wanted to see what he saw, my arse closing around the head of his cock, the skin around my hole puckering up as he pulled back. "Next time."

"Let's get your first time done first." He pushed back in a little further this time. "God, you're still tight."

"No, you're big."

"You do know how to flatter, kid." He gave me another inch. "Is it your first threesome?"

Threesome?

Oh, yes. Him, me, and Baby Doll. Mustn't forget Baby Doll. I had, for a moment. Hadn't been able to think about anything but that thick cock working its way up inside me. But now I remembered that Rod was fucking me over the bonnet of that lovely, lovely car. My fantasy come true. "Done threesomes. And moresomes."

Rod gave me another inch, almost faster than I could handle. "Well, one moresome," I admitted. "Not like this, though."

"And here I was thinking that my baby doll was your first love." He reached down and squeezed my balls again. "And you didn't save yourself for her."

"Too bloody scared to ever make a move," I confessed. "Thought you'd skin me alive if you caught me."

"Well, I'm glad you waited." A little more cock inside me, making me wonder how much more there was of it. "You looked pretty hot, feeling her up." More cock. "And I'm certainly not complaining about how tight you are. Even if means I have to be careful." One more careful thrust, feeding the length of that cock into me. "Did I use enough of that cream on you?"

Baby Doll's beauty cream worked up inside me. "Yeah." He was almost too big for me, but only almost. "Wanna give...her some cream...too..." Needed it now. Rod had paused just long enough for me to cope with the size of his cock filling me up. Now I wanted more. Wanted him to fuck my brains out, his weight crushing my cock against Baby Doll.

I let go of my arse and pulled my arms round to stretch out full length over the bonnet, turning my head so I could rest my mouth against it, kissing that smooth paint work.

"You are such a pretty sight, son." Rod pulled back a little and then shoved back in, making my cock slap against Baby Doll. "Just keep kissing her. I'll take care of you both."

He pulled further back the next time, giving me a longer stroke. Then almost all the way out, and hard in, making me feel the size of him. Almost too much, almost, but I stayed where I was. Because another few strokes would do it, and I'd be coming all over his lovely car.

Then he hammered into me like a piston, and for one last giddy moment, I wondered what would become of me. Because I was going to come, couldn't stop it now, and he was older than me. Old enough that maybe he'd just keep hammering away when I was done and couldn't move.

"Tell her how much you love her," he said, and I realised I was moaning into the hot metal under me. "Tell her how much you want her and her daddy to fuck you together."

So I told her and her daddy, "Want you both to fuck me. Want to come between you..."

And as I said it, I knew that I would. Rod slammed into me, squeezing my come out of me. My cream all over my pretty girl's bonnet to replace the cream Rod had used on me.

All I could do was hold on tight for the ride, let Rod hold me down on that car and fuck me until he'd fucked out everything I had left to come with. Pinned between car and man, nothing to do but enjoy how it felt to come, a spurt from me with each stroke from him. My own come wet between me and Baby Doll, letting my cock slip smoothly over her as her daddy kept pounding into my arse.

And then I was done, and I would have slid down to the ground if Rod hadn't been holding me up. Instead, I was content to lie there and let him finish inside me, another three or four long strokes, the last almost pulling right out, before he shoved it back in and held still. He was so damn big I couldn't help but feel the pulse of his cock as he came.

Then he did pull right out and pulled away from me. I levered myself to my feet, remembering my shorts just in time to avoid tripping myself with them. I kept on my feet just long enough to step out of the shorts and take a step or two back to the grass behind me and sat down before I fell. Then I lay back, found myself staring straight into the sun, and flung up an arm to cover my face.

"Not maidenly modesty at this stage?"

"No, just got the sun in my eyes."

I felt a shadow fall across me, sudden coolness where it blocked out the sun. I opened my eyes and looked up to find Rod standing in front of me. I was still a little sun-dazzled, but not so much I didn't get an eyeful of his cock. Even now, looking a little softer than it had a few minutes ago, it was enormous. "Bloody hell, how did that all fit?"

"Practice. More on my part than on yours, it seems." He sat down beside me. "You really do have a thing for that car, don't you?"

Since he'd noticed that while fucking me senseless, I refused to be embarrassed about it. "Isn't that why you asked me round to do her?"

"Yeah." He put a hand out and stroked my chest. "Didn't expect to actually do more than watch you enjoy groping her, though. Well, mostly."

I rolled over to face him. "Don't be modest. It's not very believable coming from someone with a slit in the back of his suit for the dorsal fin."

He flicked a finger under my chin. "Listen, kid, you're a neighbour. I might like the way you've filled out since you went away to uni, but you're still living at home with your mum and dad, and I'd have some explaining to do if they thought I was corrupting their little boy. I'd have been happy just to watch you trying to keep one hand off your cock while you've got the other hand on her." He nodded at the car. "And you'd better go and rinse her off. You don't need to finish the job I paid you for, not just yet, but don't let that stain set on her."

Pretending to grumble, I started to get to my feet. Then I realised that I still had my boxers around my thighs. I could pull them up, but Rod might just laugh at more maidenly modesty, so I pulled them right off before getting up.

I just had time to turn the hose on the mess I'd made of Baby Doll, before I realised that I might need the same service for the same mess Rod had made of me. He'd put plenty of lube into me, and now I was standing up, it was starting to make its presence felt.

I was feeling pretty squelchy by the time I'd rinsed Baby Doll's bonnet, even though that didn't take very long. Rod must have noticed, because he came up behind me, took the hose from my hand, and used it on me.

"Hey!" It wasn't that cold, and it wasn't that forceful, but it still made me jump to have water suddenly bubbling over my hole.

"Just getting you cleaned up a bit before you sit on my clean lounger." He turned up the pressure of the stream of water, just a little, but enough to get my attention. "Though if you like it, we can play around a bit later."

That was getting just a little too kinky for me, at least for one day. "I'll stick with using it on her for now."

"Fine." He turned the water down to a trickle and then off, leaving me wet but a lot less sticky. "You'll dry off pretty quickly in this heat. Come and have a beer."

I followed him over to the patio, flopped onto the spare lounger, and accepted a can and glass. A couple of swigs, because I really did need a drink, and then I set down the beer, closed my eyes, and lay back, basking in the sun.

I WAS WOKEN from a light doze by something dropping softly across my lap. "Huh?"

"You'll get sunburnt if you leave it hanging out like that. And I don't think you'd like that."

I suddenly remembered where I was and what I'd been doing. Rod was right; I wouldn't like sunburn there at all. "Would you kiss it better for me?"

He laughed and said, "Maybe. But I think you should finish the car first. Actually, finish your beer first."

Good idea. I drained half the glass without thinking about it, and I realised I was genuinely thirsty from the heat. "I could probably do with some water." And a snack.

As if reading my mind, Rod said, "I bet you haven't eaten a proper lunch. Come inside and grab something from the fridge."

What had fallen across my cock was my own shorts, so I pulled them on and followed Rod inside. Maybe I should have stopped to put on the boxers first, because the heavier fabric of the shorts was pulling over my cock in a way I couldn't quite ignore, especially when I was looking at the way Rod's shorts pulled tight over his arse with each stride. But I'd had a good fucking only...I glanced at my watch...half an hour ago, and I didn't *need* more right now, even if I wouldn't mind more. So I just enjoyed the view and thought about having Rod for dessert.

A bit of cheese and bread should be enough to keep me going until dinner. Having collected them, I sat down a little gingerly on a hard kitchen chair, but nothing seemed to hurt too much. Rod had handled me as carefully as he would Baby Doll, and I knew I could take that cock again with no trouble at all. I had every intention of doing so, but for now, I was content to watch as Rod bustled about the kitchen putting on the kettle.

As I finished the sandwich, Rod set a mug of tea in front of me. "Here. We can stay here or take it out to the garage." He sat down across the table from me. "We could do with being out of the sun for a bit, and the rest of the shampoo and set can wait."

We were both fairly well tanned, but he was probably right. Besides, I wouldn't mind seeing what was new in the garage. "Got any new toys?"

He looked at me with a slight smile.

"I didn't mean it like that!"

"No, you didn't. But, yes, I do." He got to his feet again and walked towards the door into the hall. "No, stay there," he added as I started to stand up.

So I sat back down, wondering what he was up to. I didn't have long to wait. He came back a minute or two later with a bag. From it, he produced a tube of lube and a butt plug. "Think you can handle that?"

I looked at it. It was crystal clear, obviously a hard plastic, no give in it. And it was big, the shaft nearly as thick as Rod, with a spherical bulge near the base that was even thicker, just before it narrowed down into the neck that would let my hole hold it in place.

"Yes," I heard my mouth say before my brain could point out that maybe I shouldn't be greedy.

"Then I think we'll go and bend you over the workbench before we finish our tea." Rod dropped his toys back into their bag, picked up his mug, and headed outside.

I followed, mostly thinking about that plug filling my arse. But just a little bit of thought left over for what Rod might have been up to while I'd been away this last term. The garage was a cave of wonders, the place where Rod worked on restoring his venerable cars to their former glory. A warm den in winter, when the doors were closed and the heater on. But a cool and shady retreat today.

Shady enough that I had to stop and blink the sun dazzle away before I could see the tools hung neatly on the pegboard rack and the current recipient of Rod's loving care parked over the work pit. But the work bench was under the window where it would be well-lit. I had no trouble at all seeing Rod patting the bench top. "Bend over."

"I'm getting the lube job today?"

"Yeah." He picked up the small bottle of light oil and then set it down again. "But I think I'll stick to the pharmaceutical-grade stuff for you."

He hadn't out by Baby Doll, but then Baby Doll's finishing wax was probably a bit more human compatible. The lube for humans would do nicely. I joined Rod, dropped my trousers, and leaned on the bench. My cock was already hard, had been for a couple of minutes now. I wanted to push it against something, but the bench didn't have Baby Doll's sweet curves.

Rod cupped my balls and rolled them a little. "Ah, the energy of youth." He let go of my balls and ran his thumb over my hole. "Still, this should keep you going until I feel like having seconds. Spread your cheeks so I've got a good view of it going in."

Yeah, Rod obviously liked watching a small hole take a large cock. Or anything else that happened to be handy. There were other tools in the garage I wouldn't mind him working on me with, although that could wait for another day.

I did as I was told and waited for a few seconds. Then I felt cold slickness as Rod pushed the butt plug against me. Against me, and then into me, the first couple of inches sliding in smoothly. Then another inch or two; in fact, the whole length up to that bulge, because suddenly I could feel it resting against me.

Back out, and then in again, Rod fucking my arse with just that length of plastic. After a few strokes, it was more than enough to keep me hot and bothered, but not quite enough to let me come hands-free. I could grab my cock, but after a year at uni, I'd started to learn that some things were worth waiting for. So I waited and held my cheeks apart for Rod's viewing pleasure and thought about Rod thinking about me.

All the way out, and then back in again, and more cool wetness. He was really getting me lubed up, and I wasn't sorry for it, thinking about the size of that bulge at the end of the plug. He was going to take it slowly; I just knew it. Watching the way that ball spread my hole right out and then narrow again as it went all the way in.

And I was right. The very next stroke, he started easing the whole thing into me. I tried to relax and let it happen, focus on how good it felt. I'd seen it, and I knew I could take it, however huge it felt right now. Stretching my entrance wide, stretching me open. Slowly, twisting a little, making me feel every millimetre. Each little twist pulling me wider, until I wondered if I really had misjudged what I could handle.

And just as I thought that, the widest part was inside, and the whole thing slipped forward a little faster, my arse sucking it in before Rod got control of it again. It was spreading me wide from inside, wider than any cock I'd taken yet. Wider even than Rod. But only for a short length, and I could manage that. Wanted more of it now, wanted the whole thing inside me, filling me up.

Rod gave it to me, a little at a time. Finally I had the lot, my hole clamping down around that narrow neck between the ball and the base plate.

And then Rod slapped me lightly across the arse and said, "Okay, you can pull your shorts up now."

"Hey!"

"I told you it was just to keep you ready for when I feel like fucking you again." He cupped my balls again. "Of course, if you'd rather just walk around the garage with everything hanging out, you're welcome to do so. Just don't complain if you get splinters when you sit down."

So I squatted down to pull up my shorts—and nearly fell over as the plug made itself felt. Getting me right on the prostate first time, and I damn near came. Would definitely have fallen over if Rod's strong hands hadn't been under my arms to hold me steady. Except that gave me time to notice just how that big bulge filled me up.

"I like a man falling at my feet," Rod said, "but give yourself a minute to get used to it."

So I held still, leaning back against Rod's legs for support until I could think straight again. When I was reasonably certain I could stand without swaying, I put one hand to the waistband of my shorts and the other hand on the bench to lever myself to my feet. I could manage by myself, but I asked anyway. "Help me up?"

"Sure." He hauled me to my feet and then let go of me so that I could turn around to face him. "Can't figure you out, kid. One moment I think you're not much past a virgin and then the next I think you must have spent every night last term getting fucked senseless, instead of wasting time drinking." He paused and grinned. "Though maybe that was just me and my friends, and the youth of today are more sensible."

"Lots of sex," I said. "Just not a lot of variety." I focused on doing up my fly. The butt plug was still making itself felt with every small movement, making it hard to think. But what I realised now was that I liked the idea of that shifting pressure teasing me for the next few minutes, keeping me near the edge without giving me relief. "And definitely not with cars." I reached out and put my hand over Rod's crotch, feeling the hardness there. He could fuck me right now if he wanted, but obviously what he wanted was to watch me squirm first. I'd be happy to play along with that. "Or with anything the size of that."

He grinned at me. "Anyone would think you were a size queen."

Well, the size of Rod's cock certainly didn't push him down my top ten list of men to be fucked by. But it wasn't the only thing I liked about him. "It's the size of your car collection I really like."

"Well, go and have a look at the new girl." He nodded at the car parked a few feet away.

She was definitely new; I didn't remember seeing her before. "Another one? Baby Doll will get jealous." I walked over to inspect the car, each step making me aware of just how big that butt plug was.

"I'm just restoring this one. When I'm done, I'll sell her on to someone who'll appreciate her but doesn't have the skill or space to clean her up." He followed me. Stood behind me, so close I could feel the heat of his body. Reached round and laid his hand over my cock. "I was going to ask you anyway if you wanted to give me some help this summer; you're old enough that I can trust you to work on her yourself and not just pass me the next spanner." He squeezed my cock. "It can be just assistant mechanic. If that's all you want."

I leaned back against him, enjoying the skin-to-skin contact of my back against his chest. "No, it's not all I want. Just as long as I do get to play with your harem, as well as you."

"I think we can arrange that." He was working my cock through my shorts now. Not tightly, not enough to let me come. But still enough to make me tense up and clamp down on that bloody butt plug.

I jerked in his arms, and that rubbed my cock against his hand and against the rough cloth of my shorts between us. Okay, maybe Rod was into dominance games, and some other day I'd be happy to let him make me wait, but right now I needed release. "Let go if you don't want me to come right now!"

"Easy, lad." He let go of my cock, although only to clamp his arm around my waist. "If you're that wound up, we'd better get on with it. Let's go back outside." Then he let go of me and stepped back so that we weren't pressed skin to skin.

I leaned on the car for a few seconds, trying to get my body under control. Mostly succeeding, but knowing I really couldn't hold out much longer. Then I straightened up and turned to face Rod. He was waiting patiently, watching me closely but letting me decide if I was fit to move. I took a step or two forward to test. "Okay, I think I can walk without falling over." Only just, because even that much movement made the plug shift inside me, stroking me and stretching me with each tiny change in my balance.

He grinned. "After you."

Because he wanted to watch me, watch the way I stumbled a little with each prod of that piece of plastic filling me up. Let him watch. I'd get my reward as soon as we made it outside and over to Baby Doll.

But Rod made it to her before I did, moving ahead of me with a few paces to go. He opened the back door and pulled out the car blanket that lay neatly folded on the back seat. "This has a decent waterproof lining." He unfolded it and draped it over the near end of the seat so that part of the seat was covered, but there was a good pad of material on the ground by the car.

It was pretty bloody obvious what came next. I dropped my shorts around my ankles, stepped out of them, and went to kneel by the car, leaning forward on the seat. The blanket did a good enough job of protecting my knees from the gravel and should do a good enough job of protecting Baby Doll's leather hide from me.

Beautiful leather it was, too. I knew that well enough. I'd given it tender loving care more than once. Snatched the chance to sniff that heady scent.

Well, now I didn't have to worry about what Rod would think if he caught me getting high on the smell of Baby Doll's seat. I dropped right down onto the seat and got a good lungful.

I knew what I must look like, sprawled across Baby Doll's back seat with my arse bare and the handle of the butt plug sticking out. I didn't care. The only one to see was Rod, and I didn't think he'd be laughing at me. All I cared about was the way that plug felt inside me and the way the woollen blanket felt against my bare cock. I didn't bother waiting for Rod but thrust against the seat.

The blanket might be wool, but it was fine and soft, and it felt bloody good as I stroked myself off against it. The butt plug felt even better, shifting with every movement.

At least until Rod lay a heavy hand on my arse and said, "Keep still while I get that out."

I didn't want to. I wanted to keep thrusting. I'd happily get off on just the blanket and Baby Doll's scent. But Rod leaned a little more weight on me, and I kept still. I focused on the way the plug felt as he slipped it out, how good it felt as the heavy ball stretched me again and then slipped free.

I felt empty for a moment, feeling where the plug had been and wasn't any more. But Rod fixed that, shoving his cock into me.

No slow inching his way in this time. No, this time he gave me the lot in one go. I could never have taken it like that the first time; he'd have left me aching and raw, but now it just felt good. Felt *right*.

Felt even better when he pulled almost all the way out and then slammed in again, pressing me hard against the blanket. This was even better than the first time, just good, solid fucking with a good solid cock, Rod's balls slapping against me at the end of the stroke.

Then another long stroke, and Rod grunted, "Damn this is good."

Almost too good, at least for me. "Can't hold out much longer."

"Don't worry, kid." Another stroke, putting me right on the brink. "You're still tight enough that I'll feel it when you come."

Another stroke of that thick cock inside me, thrusting my cock in turn against the delicate roughness of the blanket. And that was enough. As Rod pulled back for his next thrust, I knew I was going over the edge. He shoved into me, and I shoved my nose into Baby Doll's leather and let loose all over the blanket.

Damn, but that felt good. Second time in an hour, in the threesome of my fantasies. Cock wet and sticky under me, arse clamping down around a thick cock. I was high on the fantasy, and I rode it all the way down, savouring every last pulse of my cock until I finished coming.

Rod hadn't been kidding. He was already coming as I finished, that thick cock quivering in my arse. Not bad for a man old enough to be my father. Though he could have kept on fucking me for another hour for all I cared at that point, because I was wrung dry and didn't care about anything at all, as long as nobody was expecting me to actually do anything but lie there.

Finally he pulled out. I wouldn't have minded lying there a while longer, but it was an awkward position, kneeling into the car. I levered myself out and up and staggered the few feet to the lawn, where I promptly collapsed in a happy, fucked-out puddle.

Rod followed me, dragging the blanket with him. He spread it out on the grass, and I rolled onto it without bothering to get up, more or less managing to avoid the wet patch I'd left on it. The sun was warm on my back, and I was content to lie there for a while, not moving even when Rod lay down next to me.

It must have been a good ten minutes before either of us moved. Then I rolled on my side to look at Rod. He cranked an eye open and looked back. "Happy, kid?"

"Mmm. We doing this again?"

"If you want. Or if you just want to work on the cars, we can do that too." He grinned. "I really didn't expect this. And I really could do with some help on the cars this summer. I was always going to ask if you wanted to earn a bit of money handing me the right spanner on the weekends."

"I'd like that." Never mind the sex, apprentice mechanic was a good way to take a necessary break from the books and earn a bit of cash. "I reckon it's going to be a long, hot summer, and we might as well make the most of it."

"Me too, kid. Me too."

Acknowledgements:

I've been writing for twenty years, and the stories in this collection were scattered over some fifteen of those years. There are a good many people who've given me advice and encouragement over that time; too many to thank individually. Even by groups I'll forget somebody, but many of the people I met along the way hung out in places like rasfc, Speculations, Absolute Write, Erosworkshop and Space City. Oh, and alt.fan.pratchett. Thank you all.

Publication acknowledgments:

Gone Fishing first published in *Mythic Fantasies*, Amatory Ink, 2002

Naked first published in *Ultimate Gay Erotica 2005*, Alyson, 2004

One Size Fits All first published in *Fishnet Magazine*, Blowfish, 2004

A Sparrow Flies Through first published in *The Mammoth Book of Quick and Dirty Erotica*, Constable & Robinson, 2013

If I Offered Thee a Bargain first published in *Forbidden Fruit*, publisher Fiona Glass, 2007

Any Port in a Storm first published in *The Mammoth Book of Urban Erotic Confessions*, Constable & Robinson, 2014

Car Wash was previously self-published, 2013

About the Author

Storm Duffy has a number of erotica shorts published under that and other names in a variety of venues, including "The Mammoth Book of Quick and Dirty Erotica". As Jules Jones, she has written several erotic romance novellas and novels, including the first M/M romance published by Loose Id.

Amongst the 2500 or so books on shelves in her house, there is room for rather a lot of cross-stitch thread and entirely too many balls of wool. There are also more bits of computer kit than is quite reasonable for someone who doesn't do that for a living. The two microscopes, on the other hand, are entirely in keeping with a career in science.

Email: jules.jones@gmail.com and storm.duffy@gmail.com

Website: www.stormduffy.com and

http://www.authorgraph.com/authors/StormDuffy

Twitter: https://twitter.com/StormDuffy

Goodreads: https://www.goodreads.com/JulesJones

Also by this author

A Collision with Reality

Also Available from NineStar Press

www.ninestarpress.com

www.ingramcontent.com/pod-product-compliance
Lightning Source LLC
Chambersburg PA
CBHW030617130626
46552CB00002B/607